Veil of Confusion

A Kessler Effect Novel

Vannetta Chapman

Cover design: Streetlight Graphics

Printed in the United States of America.

First printing, 2022

ASIN: B0BHV4QJ54

ISBN: 9798362783310

Contents

Dedicated to Peggy Looper

"But if I go to the east, he is not there;
If I go to the west, I do not find him."
Job 23:8

"Though much is taken, much abides; and though
We are not now that strength which in old days
Moved earth and heaven, that which we are, we are."
~Alfred Lord Tennyson

Chapter 1

T HEY WERE UP WELL before the sun. The items they would take with them had been laid out, sorted, packed, and then sifted through again and repacked. What could be left? What would they need?

Winter items on the bottom.

Food near the top.

Weapons in their pockets.

They'd prepared the night before and the night before that. Harper didn't think they'd be able to sleep their last night in the old bus. She had thought they'd lie awake staring at the ceiling, imagining all that could go wrong. But she and Cade had both fallen immediately into the place of dreams and memories and hope.

They woke early. They always woke early, before the wild dogs had begun their foraging. There was little more to do than slip into their clothes and wait for the moment to shoulder their packs.

Cade had lit the single lantern and turned it to low. Harper drank in his profile—his strong jawline, warm brown eyes, slightly crooked nose. The nose helped him to fit into their world. No one should have movie-star looks, and Cade's nose saved him from that. But it was his hands that caused a lump to rise in her throat. It was his hands that were scarred, strong, capable, tender.

"We should eat something." He pulled out a piece of the hard bread they'd cooked in the campfire using a Dutch oven the day before, broke it in half, and handed it to her. "Would you like some butter with that?"

"And jam. Strawberry please."

Neither smiled at the old joke. It had passed between them so many times that now it felt like sand slipping through their fingers.

Harper continued watching Cade as she attempted to chew the tack. Studying him, it seemed she could trace the path of their lives since June 6th. His arms had grown stronger and tan, and his hair long. The beard came in thick with a bit of gray—something that had surprised them both. His shoulders seemed broader to her, though she supposed that was impossible. One's physique didn't change because of the burdens you were forced to carry.

And yet they had changed—irrevocably.

Those first weeks of June weren't something she cared to dwell on. The violence and terror and swiftness with which they'd descended into lawlessness. If she thought on those things, she was filled with a despair that threatened to strangle her.

Instead, she tried to call to mind the man she'd fallen in love with three months earlier and found she couldn't. The face she stared at now was the only one she knew. It showed his abiding love for her, his concern for what they were about to attempt, and the strain of a life lived in El Paso's northern barrio—otherwise known as *Lugar de Los Muertos*, or *Muertos Norte* for short.

Harper preferred northern barrio.

Cade pulled out his canister of filtered water, unscrewed the top, and passed it to her. The water was cold and a little gritty. The filters didn't catch everything, but if the water was going to kill her it probably would have done so by now. Harper drank her fill, passed it back to Cade, and watched as he guzzled the rest.

Then he stood and refilled it from the collection tank. A pipe fitted into the ceiling of the bus collected rain water, which in far west Texas was precious little. The water slid through the pipe, passed the two sets of filters, and settled into the collection tank, which was actually an old galvanized stock tank. Cade had walked an entire day looking for that tank. He'd searched a dozen abandoned farms on the outskirts of town.

His water purification system was just one reason the bus would be claimed before they'd reached the edge of the barrio.

Harper peeked through a slit in the blackout curtains. A crescent moon dipped toward the horizon. She watched until she was able to see the outline of the Franklin Mountains, then nodded to Cade, and he doused the light. They left the bus more silently than the sun approached the horizon. They walked west.

Tía lived in a former FEMA trailer. The words were emblazoned on the side, though they'd faded in the harsh Texas sun. Harper didn't know how old Tía was but would have guessed her to be in her eighties. She also didn't know if the woman was Hispanic or Native American, though ethnicities had ceased to matter long ago. She didn't even know if Tía had once had children or grandchildren. She lived alone and spoke only rarely of her life before.

Everyone called her Tía, and if there was a leader in the northern barrio, she was it.

No one entered the barrio without her approval.

No one dared to leave it without her blessing.

The rumors surrounding Tía were as numerous and varied as cacti in the desert. She'd healed a boy. She'd raised a woman from the dead. Her entire family had been killed in the fall. She'd always lived alone. She was a prophet or an empath or possibly a former spy.

Tía was sitting on the porch of her trailer, stroking an old tabby cat. How she managed to feed herself, let alone the cat, was a mystery. Harper suspected people dropped off a portion of what little they had, like sacrifices left on the steps of the Greek gods in hopes of finding favor.

"Cade and Harper, it is good to see you."

Cade threw a glance at Harper. Tía had been blind for at least as long as she'd lived in the northern barrio. How she knew it was them was yet another mystery. Perhaps the loss of her sight had sharpened her other senses. It was possible that they walked differently or smelled differently.

"What you have to tell me is best said inside." She gently set the cat on the ground, then pushed to her feet and led them into the single room that was her home.

One long wall of the trailer was fitted with shelves, and on those shelves sat hundreds of jars. Anyone who found a jar unshattered brought it to Tía. In turn, she filled them with herbs that she grew in the small plot of ground beside her trailer. That plot of ground was probably better guarded than the entire barrio. People depended on Tía's herbs for medical problems, emotional problems, even spiritual problems. Harper didn't know where the seeds had come from or how, given her blindness, Tía was able to tell one jar from another.

Once inside, Tía sat in the rocker and the cat jumped back onto her lap. "So, you're leaving?"

"Yes." Cade perched on the edge of the couch and Harper did the same. "We wanted to say goodbye and to thank you...for everything."

"You both have served an important role in our little community. The barrio will miss you, but your destiny does not lie here."

Harper let out a breath. She hadn't realized, until that moment, how much Tía's blessing meant to her.

"Which direction will you go?"

"North, through the Franklin Mountains." Cade stared at his hands. "We know to stay away from major roads."

Tía nodded and set the chair to rocking, studying the cat as her hand brushed it from head to tail, head to tail. Finally, she raised her head and offered a smile. Harper thought it was one of the most beautiful things she'd seen in a very long while—Tía's smiling face, lined with the wrinkles of fate and time, her dark skin weathered to the texture of soft leather, still-mostly-black hair braided and pulled over her left shoulder.

"I am sure you have given this considerable thought. No doubt you are as prepared as two *viajeros* can be." She again stroked the cat. "But you should go east, not north."

"East?" Harper's voice broke on the word. "There's nothing...east."

"Exactly. You will travel un-accosted."

"I don't understand." Cade laced his fingers together, elbows propped on his knees, and leaned forward. "We need to go north. How will going east—"

Tía held up a weathered hand. "The Guadalupe Mountains are full of caves, springs, even old cabins. The Mescalero Apache lived there for many years, and after that the white men came, looking first for water and later for oil."

"McKittrick Canyon." Cade scrubbed a hand over his face. "I've been there once, but, Tía..." The next words were offered gently, nearly a plea. "We need to go north."

"Climb the mountains to the east. You have your spy glass, yes?"

Cade hesitated, glanced at Harper, and finally nodded. Harper wondered again how the old blind woman could be aware of their silent communication, because Tía waited for that nod, then continued.

"You will be able to see a great distance in every direction from Guadalupe Peak. Possibly you will even see your future. And if there is danger and destruction, as you fear, you will see that too."

Cade looked to Harper then and waited for her response. Harper didn't know Tía's history or what gifts she actually possessed, but she was certain that her words had the ring of truth to them. She nodded once, and it was decided. They would abandon the route they'd so carefully planned. Instead, they would walk east.

Chapter 2

C ADE WATCHED TÍA AGAIN struggle to her feet. He had no doubt she would have slapped his hand away if he'd attempted to help. This woman represented so much to so many people, but for Cade she epitomized two things—the past and the future. If there was anything in their collective past worth remembering, it was Tía and all she stood for. And if there was anything in their future to hope for, it was also her and her ability to see a path through the veil of confusion that surrounded them.

Tía represented kindness and truth and compassion more than it seemed a single person could. She had somehow survived the horror of the previous months, and she'd kept those qualities intact. In fact, they shone brightly from her person like starlight piercing a pitch-black sky.

She stopped in front of Harper and placed both of her hands on his wife's head. It should have been a funny sight—though Harper was sitting and Tía was standing they were practically the same height. But it wasn't funny. It touched Cade's heart at its core and caused an ache that he might once have considered a heart attack.

Harper was young and strong and vibrant.

Tía was old, fragile, full of a quiet wisdom.

She was nearing the end of her life on this earth, less than one hundred pounds, and helpless if judged by the ways of the world.

She closed her eyes and spoke in an old tongue, one Cade didn't recognize but thought might be a combination of Hispanic and Apache. As he watched, tears slid down Harper's face and a smile spread across Tía's. Finally, she leaned forward, kissed Harper's forehead and wished her Godspeed.

Harper stood, looked at them both, then whispered, "I'll wait outside."

Tía sat beside him on the couch. "You are a strong man, Cade. Strong with a quick mind and a good heart. That's a rare combination."

His pulse raced as he anticipated what she would say next because her expression had changed to one of grave concern.

"Harper is also strong, but she needs you, Cade. You must protect her. You must protect the child that grows within her. You must see that they both reach a land where the child may thrive. Traveling east will be slower, but speed is not your goal. Your goal is to see those two settled in a safe section, and though you believe that to be New Mexico, it is not."

How had she known their final destination?

How had she known Harper was pregnant? They'd told no one, and she'd yet to experience any morning sickness. Only eight weeks along, she wasn't showing yet. If he hadn't been a doctor in the former world, he might have missed the signs himself.

"Look at me, Cade. Do you understand how important this is?"

"Yes." The single word seemed to catch in his throat, and he made no attempt to stop the tears coursing down his face. Their destination had been Cloudcroft, or at least that area. He'd heard the rumor more than once—a small group beginning a new community in Lincoln National Forest. He was determined to find them.

"Go east."

"But north is where we need to be. East will more than double our distance."

"If you go east, you will arrive where you need to be before winter sets in."

"By then Harper will be in her second trimester."

"Go east, Cade. Stay in the canyons until you're sure it's safe to travel farther. Should I be wrong—and yes, I have been wrong before—you can still make Cloudcroft by late spring, early summer at the latest."

"But if we go north—"

She covered his hands with hers. They were small, brown, ancient. "If you go north, you will not make it at all."

He didn't answer.

He didn't know how to answer.

"Your way east will be difficult, and there will be times..." She turned away, stared at something on the far wall of the trailer and swiped at her own cheeks. When she turned back, her face glowed with an expression of calm resolve. She again reached for his hands. Clasped them. "It's possibly the most important thing you'll ever do, but I have faith in you, Cade."

He nodded once—finally giving in to this new reality with the same stoicism he'd accepted the fall of his old world. Then they both stood and he embraced her. It was like putting his arms around a bird. He felt the breath go out of her as she sighed, and it washed over him reminding him of the time he was twelve and had been baptized in the Brazos River.

When she stepped away, he cinched up his pack, thanked her one more time, and stepped outside.

Harper turned, studied him, then nodded once.

They set out for the east side of the barrio.

It was no problem leaving the barrio. Many left to scavenge for food or weapons or clothing. Those finds had become increasingly rare, but people still searched. Their leaving would not raise suspicions. The packs they carried might. Harper was adept at telling a lie so that it rang of truth. It was one reason she'd been a bestselling author. Now she used her skill to talk her way past the guard at the east wall.

"Morning, Cade. Harper."

"Liam."

Cade shook the man's hand as Harper adjusted the straps on her pack—purposely drawing Liam's attention to it. Liam Contreras was tall with a bushy beard that seemed to fan out in all directions. His hair had grown long and was pulled up in a topknot. He seemed affable, even seemed like someone they could trust.

But how could they know for sure?

It's possibly the most important thing you'll ever do...

"Why are you two up and about so early? And why are you going out this way? Nothing but desert. No one's passed through this gate—coming or going—in over a month. I'm not sure why we still bother to guard it."

"It's my fault." Harper stared at her feet. When she glanced up, Cade was surprised to see her blushing. "I need a few hours free of..."

She looked back the way she had come, her lower lip trembling. Blinking back her tears, she cleared her throat, then continued. "I told Cade if I didn't get out of the barrio for a couple hours, I was going to pull every last strand of hair out of my head."

Harper's hair was a rich auburn and fell down her back in a braid that reached to her waist.

"That would be a shame." Liam looked embarrassed by her tears. He adjusted the strap of the M-16 rifle.

Rifles had been issued to every guard in the barrio. They'd found a cache of them in a home on the south side the first week after the 6th of June. The rifle was simple to operate, lightweight, and packed a punch.

"If anyone's earned a free morning, you two have. Not much to see out this direction, though."

Cade stepped closer to Harper, slipped a hand around her waist. "We're turning back north. Didn't want the little ones to see us and try to follow."

The children of the barrio were largely unsupervised during daylight hours. It was true that they would shadow a person anywhere, especially if that person was Dr. Cade. He'd developed something of a cult following.

"Makes sense. Well, don't get lost out there."

Which caused them all to laugh because Cade often led the scouting parties that went in search of supplies. Summers spent in Colorado, hiking the mountains with his father, had given him two of his most valued skills—the ability to read maps as well as an uncanny knowledge of exactly where they were at any given time. It had been on one of those recent scouting trips that he'd first had the idea of leaving, after Harper had shared she was pregnant.

Liam opened the gate. The metal hinges groaned.

Cade and Harper slipped through.

They turned north, past houses marked with the barrio's symbol. A large X on the left side, facing the street, chest high, indicated the place had been searched for anything of value. They'd stopped searching for people months ago.

"I didn't realize so many of the homes were burned."

"Those not willing to come into the city proper tried to survive on their own."

Which was exactly what they were doing.

Only it wasn't. They were headed toward a new group, a better one than the barrio they were leaving behind.

They were headed toward their future.

El Paso was their past.

Cade felt a weight lift off him. Being free of the barrio's fence and his responsibilities there eased the tension in his shoulders. He should have known that he couldn't do it alone, though that had been his first reaction to whatever had happened on the 6th of June. Initially, he tried to continue working at the hospital. When that became impossible, he decided to survive in their new world alone. He'd known it would be difficult—almost impossible, but there was nothing left to do other than try as hard as he could for as long as he could.

But now there was Harper.

And the baby.

He noticed Harper put her hands in her pockets and knew that she was gripping the handles of both handguns. "You okay?"

"Of course." She shrugged, then offered him a crooked smile. "Meetings with Tía are always a bit...unsettling."

He nodded and found himself grateful that she hadn't heard the entire conversation with the old woman. Neither suggested ignoring Tía's advice. They walked north until he felt they were far enough away from anyone guarding the watchtowers to see, and then they turned east. Twice he thought he heard someone behind them. They paused, pulled out their binoculars, watched and waited.

"I guess we're a little jumpy." Harper handed the binoculars to him, but instead of storing them in his pack, he slipped the strap over his head and let them dangle from the leather cord, tucking them inside his jacket. El Paso's weather tended toward unbearably hot, and though it was late September he'd be shedding the jacket before noon.

He led them south and east, avoiding the larger roads when possible and the interstate at all cost. He didn't need to consult the map. He knew the streets of El Paso as well as he knew the backyard of his childhood home. He'd done his residency in El Paso, then stayed on when the Children's Hospital had offered him a permanent position. Those first few years, when he'd needed a break from the pressure and heavy case load, he'd taken his motorcycle to the streets—riding through, around, and beyond El Paso.

Cade had set a fast walking pace that he fully realized they couldn't maintain. The goal was to get them to the outskirts of El Paso before they stopped. He estimated they'd gone a dozen miles in five hours. Normally, that would be an easy pace, but not with the packs they were carrying.

It was challenging, exhausting, grueling.

The sun was high in the sky when everything went to shit.

"Movement on the right." Harper dropped into a crouch and Cade realized it was beginning and that he'd been expecting it and that he wasn't afraid. When had he stopped being afraid? In that moment before any shots rang out, he heard Tía's words.

Harper is strong, but she needs you, Cade. You must protect her. You must protect the child that grows within her.

They'd just approached a neighborhood called Homestead Meadows, skirting north of Highway 62. The homes looked abandoned, though they didn't have the X's they'd seen closer to the barrio. He'd been here once, in the beginning, when they still had fuel for their scavenging runs. He'd found some medications in a pharmacy that had been looted.

They took up a position behind an abandoned Ford F-150. All four tires were flat and someone had ripped out the seats.

"Three to the northwest. They're holding their position." He dropped the binoculars and glanced toward Harper. She was studying the area more directly west.

"There's a larger group to the west. I count half a dozen."

The shots were a warning or a distraction. Both groups were still too far away to actually hit them. Unless they had a military rifle. Cade and Harper had automatically dropped behind the wheel wells. Now they looked at each other, an understanding passing between them. They'd gone over this scenario so many times that it felt as if they were reliving a dream.

They rose simultaneously, rising above the body of the truck just enough to peer over it.

"Assholes to the west are approaching."

"Their friends to the northwest are doing the same."

Both pulled their handguns. Cade had one in his pocket and another in his pack. He set the extra on the ground next to him and palmed the .380 he was most comfortable with. Harper had a Sig Sauer in each pocket. She set one beside her and gripped the other. There was no use firing until their targets were closer.

Maybe they wouldn't come closer.

Maybe they would peel off.

They didn't peel off.

Slowly, they advanced, carrying what looked to be a heavy piece of metal siding in front of them. Cade wouldn't have trusted his life behind it, but then what did he know? The guards had handled the bulk of their attacks. Only rarely were the other men and women in the barrio called on to provide back-up. Those events had not ended well for either side, and perhaps word had spread because they hadn't been attacked in any organized way since.

This was different.

They were no longer on their home turf.

At the same time, they weren't threatening anyone, they were simply passing through. So why the strong show of aggression? His thoughts were occasionally interrupted by the popping of a random shot that ricocheted off something nearby.

"There must be a surplus of ammo in Homestead Meadows," Cade muttered.

Harper had assumed a shooting position, and he did the same—the bulk of their body still behind the wheel wells, their forearms resting on top of the rusted frame of the truck, safeties off, their guns aimed and ready to fire.

He had the fleeting thought that often accompanied such moments.

How had it come to this?

And then the real shooting began.

Chapter 3

T HE SUDDEN VOLLEY OF gunfire stopped. The people approaching their position seemed to be regrouping, evaluating their plan of attack, sizing up the opponent.

Sizing up Harper and Cade.

Harper had not fired a pistol before the 6th of June. Even in the weeks immediately following that fateful day—a day they still didn't completely understand—she had not resorted to violence. She couldn't conceive it. The grid went down, the water stopped flowing, and the grocery shelves emptied, but she had stubbornly clung to the belief that law and order would prevail.

She abhorred violence.

Refused to write about it in her novels.

Refused to allow it in her life.

Then just when she'd thought things couldn't get any worse, they had. She'd been living in a luxury condominium on the north side. Neighbors were cautiously helpful during the first few days. When it became obvious that things would not return to normal anytime soon, that changed.

All communication from local officials ceased.

Local stores were ransacked.

Gunshots rang out at all hours of the day and night.

So, she had stuffed her essentials into a backpack, locked her door—knowing full well that someone would probably break it down before she made it out of the complex—and headed east. She'd heard from the friend of a neighbor about the northern barrio. Word on the street was that they were enclosing the area with a fence. You could only get in if you agreed to follow certain rules. It was a safe place. On her way there, she'd seen long columns of vehicles leaving Fort Bliss, driving north.

She'd circumvented the main gate to the military base, but even from a block over she could see and hear the crowds gathered there, trying to get in, demanding answers. The gates were guarded by soldiers holding rifles and staring straight ahead.

No one she spoke to knew where the tanks were going.

No one could tell her what had happened.

It was nearly dark by the time she arrived at the barrio. A tall man with brown hair and a crooked nose had been talking to a woman standing guard. He introduced himself as Cade Dawson, the camp's doctor. The guard's name was Jessica.

They'd both been kind, explaining to her that they were trying to create a safe place, trying to help each other survive this thing, trying to build a community. There was some food and water. She could sleep under a large canopy that was shared by newcomers.

Cade had offered to walk her over to it.

But first the guard had to check her pack—mainly to make sure there were no drugs.

Cade had thrown a crooked smile her way when the guard pulled out the laptop.

"Nice doorstop."

"I'm a writer—I *was* a writer."

His smile turned sympathetic. "We're all struggling to find how we fit into this world since *the fall.*"

"The fall?"

He'd shrugged. "That's what some people call it. And no, we don't know what happened. What we do know is that whatever it was seems to have caused civilized society to fall on its ass—hence the name."

One requirement of living in the barrio was that every new person meet with an old woman named Tía. If Tía agreed you could stay, then you had to pick a group to work with. Teachers for the children. Scavengers who went outside the fence. Cooks and clean-up crews and guards.

Everyone worked.

You also had to undergo an afternoon of handgun training. Another requirement was for every adult to carry a pistol at all times, to be ready at any moment to defend the barrio and the people inside the fence.

Still, Harper had clung to the illusion that she didn't have to change, that she didn't have to become someone her previous self wouldn't recognize.

The July battle had changed that. As the main contingency of the Logan Heights crew engaged their guards on the north side of the barrio, a half dozen men slipped over an undefended portion of the south wall.

She'd come around the corner as a giant of a man had scooped up a young boy in his left arm. He was carrying a rifle in his right, but he never had the chance to use it. Harper put two bullets in his chest when he'd turned toward her.

Clutching Eduardo to herself, she made sure he was uninjured, returned him to his mother, and joined the inner circle of defense. She helped to hold the line until the men and women who had rushed to back up the guards could rejoin them. She shot two more of the marauders from Logan Heights, though she couldn't be sure if it was her bullet that killed either of them.

Harper and those around her protected the children, and that was what had mattered. Suddenly, the fantasy that she might be able to deal with threats diplomatically shattered. They were living in a different world. She could get on board, or she could watch those she cared about be taken away.

And now she was protecting the man she loved.

The child not yet born.

"Who are you today?" Cade threw her a cocky smile. "Let me guess. Storm?"

"Captain America."

"That will work too."

When it was necessary for Harper to act aggressively, to respond in a way foreign to her nature, she channeled one of the Marvel Comic characters. It didn't matter which super hero she envisioned, male or female, young or old.

All that mattered was that for a moment she was able to drop the identity of Harper Moore, don the persona of a defender, and do what needed to be done. The change in her way of thinking had been disturbingly easy. Maybe that's the way things were in this post-modern world. Perhaps that was how a person's psyche was able to get up in the morning, boil water for coffee, teach children and scour for supplies and tend to the injured...all after having killed someone the night before.

Harper didn't pretend to understand the changes in the world around her or the changes in herself, but as she and Cade crouched behind the wheel wells of the burned-out truck, she knew two things for certain.

She would protect the child within her.

She would be a helpmate, not a hindrance, to Cade.

"I have no idea what they want, but they're not backing down." Cade racked the slide on his .380 semi-automatic pistol.

Harper ejected the magazine from her Sig Sauer P322, replaced it with one that was full, and slapped it back into the gun. Her pulse pounded in her ears, sweat slipped down her back, and her mind murmured that they should have stayed in the barrio.

"My group has split in two," she muttered.

"Shit."

"Exactly."

Surmising that they were up against two individuals, the Homestead Meadows welcome committee had broken into three groups, knowing Cade and Harper couldn't effectively battle against an additional front. If there'd been three people huddled on Harper's side of the truck, the Homestead Meadows group would have broken into four.

Harper pivoted—center, left, center, left.

She could feel Cade take the center when she moved left. Then he'd angle right as she took the center.

Ready for anyone who might lurch forward.

Calculating the distance between them and the time it would take for this group to cross it.

They worked together flawlessly, but it didn't make the outcome look any brighter. They held their fire, saving their ammunition until the group was within range.

Then, just as the group attacking was close enough for Harper to make out features—normal people, a bit dirty, a bit gaunt—just as she and Cade started shooting, the thought passed through her mind that they might not make it out of this one. And that was when she heard the tat-tat-tat of an M-16 set on 3-round bursts coming from a couple yards behind them.

Behind them?

The approaching attackers began shouting orders as first one, then another of their group went down. Someone made the call to retreat. The shielded group moved forward, snatched up their injured, and then quickly retreated.

Harper turned to Cade, who was glancing behind them.

She pivoted, raised her Sig, and focused her gaze down the site.

"Don't shoot me, Harper." Liam Contreras stepped out from behind a trash dumpster. "I'm on your side, remember?"

She stared at him in disbelief, finally lowering her weapon. She wasn't imagining the man who had just saved their lives. It was Liam Contreras.

Tall.

Hair pulled into a top-knot.

Bushy beard.

What was he doing here? How had he managed to circle around behind them?

"You can explain why you're here later," Cade said. "We need to move."

They continued east another mile and stopped when they reached Butternut Trail. An abandoned gas station on the north side of the road provided some cover. It was situated on a bit of a rise, providing a good view in all four directions. The structure itself had been burned out, but there were half walls to slump against, and a bit of the roof remained, providing some shade against the unrelenting sun.

Liam and Cade verified that the gas station was empty while Harper maintained a watch outside. All was quiet, deserted, eerily devoid of life.

No movement in any direction.

"All clear," Liam declared.

Cade nodded to her backpack which was on the ground. "Good time to hydrate."

"Will do, Doc." Harper's adrenaline continued to thrum through her veins. She felt like laughing, though she knew there was nothing funny about their situation. But they had survived, and some days that was enough to put a smile on your face.

They sat in a circle, more to keep a watch in opposite directions than for any other reason.

Liam pulled a large bottle of water from his pack. "I guess you have questions."

"We do," Cade said.

"As do I." Liam's smile faded, replaced by a look of concern.

"Why did you follow us?" Harper asked.

"Because I didn't buy your story."

Harper must have looked surprised, because he added, "You're not that great an actress."

"She kind of is," Cade said.

When Harper only stared at him and waited, he laughed. "Okay. You are that good of an actress, but I'd been forewarned."

Cade threw a worried look in Harper's direction. "By whom?"

"Tía."

"Wait." Harper recapped her water bottle. "Tía told you to follow us?"

"Uh-huh. Actually, she said you'd need help, but that you wouldn't ask for it. She told me to fill a pack, be ready to move, and stay out of sight until the time was right." He nodded back in the direction they had come. "Seemed like the right time when those fools were shooting at you."

Harper felt confused, muddled even. The adrenaline surge had passed, leaving her hungry and tired. Maybe those things were why she wasn't buying Liam's story. Or maybe she didn't believe him because what he was saying didn't seem possible. "When did she tell you this?"

"Last night."

Harper stared at the ground, pulling in her bottom lip and trying to think of a reasonable explanation. She couldn't. She looked at Cade, who simply shrugged. He'd always been better able to accept Tía's abilities than she had. Cade was a man of science, but he had long ago reached the opinion that some things were beyond science. Harper, on the other hand, was a skeptic in every way. Years of writing, of intense research, had taught her that most things could be explained if you took the time and effort to look hard enough. But this...

Liam had been about to bite into some tack. Instead, he slipped it back into its container. "Something wrong?"

"We didn't tell Tía that we were leaving until this morning," Cade explained. "So how did she know to tell you to follow us last night?"

"Don't ask me. I have no idea how she does what she does."

Harper leaned forward. "She just told you to pack your stuff and follow us, and you did?"

"Yeah."

"How long did you plan on doing that?"

"As long as I needed to."

"And then what?"

Liam looked slightly miffed now. He ran a hand across the top of his head, found the top knot that held his hair back and tightened the band. Finally, he said, "I guess I'd hoped that you would let me come along after I saved your ass."

"You didn't—"

"Yeah, he did, Harper." Cade held up a hand to stop the argument. He turned his attention back to Liam. "First, thank you."

Liam, always one to brush things off, nodded and said, "No problem." Then he broke off a piece of the tack and popped it into his mouth.

Harper felt unreasonably irritated, and she wasn't sure why. Liam was a standup guy. There was no doubt about whose side he was on, but his presence wasn't making any sense to her.

"It's not that I'm not grateful. I am. It's just that you don't even know where we're going, or for how long, or what we'll find there."

"I suspect you don't know those things either, except maybe the where."

She couldn't argue with him about that.

She also couldn't fathom someone just up and leaving everything behind because an old woman told him to. Though wasn't that basically what they had done?

Still, seeking Tía's blessing was one thing. Following her orders was another.

"I didn't have anything there, Harper. Okay? You think I'm going to live in the barrio the rest of my life? It's not sustainable. They're good people—mostly—but that isn't enough. They need to move out of the El Paso area, but the ruling council has considered and rejected that idea at least three times."

Harper didn't know how to answer that.

The subject of the ruling council was one she and Cade had tossed around many nights. She certainly didn't want to head back into that quagmire today.

Instead, she stood, stretched her hamstrings and quads, and took another long drink from her water bottle. "Twelve hours of sunlight, and we've burned through more than half of it. We should get going."

Liam didn't ask where they were going. Perhaps Tía had told him that as well. Or maybe it didn't matter. He wanted out of the barrio, he was following Tía's orders, and they weren't going to shake him even if they wanted to. Harper wasn't sure if they wanted to. He'd definitely been a help with the Homestead Meadows gang.

They'd figure it out later that night, or the next day, or when it needed to be figured out. Their primary focus had to be on moving east, away from the heavily populated suburbs of El Paso and out into the desert.

Chapter 4

C ADE HAD HOPED THEY could make between two and three miles an hour for eight hours on that first day—four hours in the morning and another four in the afternoon. Daylight still lasted twelve hours since they were so far south and west. He planned to spend the middle four hours, the hottest four, resting and hydrating.

Given the packs they were carrying, it was a fast pace, but he and Harper were probably in the best shape of their lives, thanks largely to no fast food, no hours spent in front of the television, and a lot of manual labor.

As for Liam, the man had a long stride and endless energy—or so it seemed after walking east for an additional four hours.

They avoided traveling on Highway 62, which would have been the most direct route. Instead, they paralleled it from the north. Maintaining that position, they would be able to hear and see anyone approaching. They'd have time to drop, though there was very little to hide behind. The desert was spotted with cacti and not much else.

They managed another seven miles after the shoot-out before Cade called it a day. They stopped in the parking area of the Flying Saucer building. Dome shaped and white it stood out against the tan colors of the desert.

"Why is this even out here?" Harper asked.

"No explaining the things that Texans will build." Cade shrugged. "Says it's private property but the place looks deserted enough."

Cade and Liam confirmed the place was unoccupied. The windows to the building had been shattered. Cade took a quick look inside, but found nothing that would be of use to them. They decided to spread out around the picnic area. More than the walking, the shoot-out and the adrenaline rush of putting El Paso behind them had been exhausting.

They ate without a campfire and agreed to a watch schedule. No one spoke of what had happened or where they were going. There simply wasn't any energy left in any of them. Lying down next to Harper, Cade immediately fell asleep.

The next day dawned cooler.

Cade felt his optimism rise. They'd made it out of El Paso. He thought the worst of any danger was behind them. He planned to set a slower but still solid pace. They were only three hours into the day's walk when they reached Hueco Ranch Road. There was a small unincorporated community to the south and east, but Cade didn't want to approach it until they had time to study it a bit. Scrub brush, cacti, and yucca plants surrounded them, and there was a sense of being able to see to the horizon.

Harper immediately sat and removed her shoes.

"You okay?"

"Yeah." She held up a shoe and dumped a handful of dirt out onto the ground. "Better now."

She attempted a smile, but Cade could tell she was tired. Harper was only five and a half feet tall, maybe a hundred and thirty pounds, twenty-nine years old with green eyes that seemed to solemnly assess everything around her. Freckles dotted the bridge of her nose and under her cheeks. She'd pulled her long auburn hair back into a single braid and wore a tan hiking hat with a wide brim that protected her face and ears from the sun.

She looked every bit as beautiful as she had the first day she'd arrived at the barrio.

Cade ran a hand over his face. He hated to waste an entire afternoon, but they needed whatever supplies might be in the homes to the south. He needed to think long-term. He couldn't afford to pass up food or water.

"Let's stop here."

Harper peered up at the sun. "We've barely started."

"Yeah, but I think we need to scout for supplies in those homes."

"And before we scout, we watch." Liam grinned. "What? I pay attention. I've been on a few of your supply runs, Cade. I'll admit I was impatient with your cautious ways at first, but it didn't take long to turn me into a believer."

They found a bit of shade thrown by a grouping of scrawny mesquite trees. Liam found a few rocks to hold down the tarp they spread out on the ground.

As if by some unspoken agreement, all three dumped out the contents of their pack. Cade and Harper had gone over and over what was essential and what they could do without. Of course, they'd been planning for two. Fortunately, Liam was pretty well equipped.

Their supplies could be divided into four basic categories—protection, non-food items, personal things, and food.

Defensive items included extra ammo, binoculars, a hunting knife, a can of pepper spray.

Nonfood things they'd packed included a weatherproof map and a compass. Cade had insisted on bringing medical supplies as well.

A first-aid kit. A surgical kit. Bottles of antibiotic pills and aspirin.

Plus general stuff. Water purification tablets, two multi-tools, a sewing kit, matches, a lightweight metal pot. He was especially pleased with the small camp stove he'd scavenged two weeks earlier. It weighed a little over two pounds and burned sticks, twigs, or scraps. Perfect for low smoke, open fire cooking. Not that they had any fresh food to cook.

The stove could also be used to heat water for the MREs or instant coffee. It was a luxury, to be sure, but one they had decided was worth the two pounds of extra weight. Lastly they had two raincoats and two tactical flashlights with extra batteries.

They'd limited personal items to two changes of clothes, a toothbrush, and a bar of soap.

As for food, they had the most basic of necessities.

Protein bars and beef jerky.

GORP that they'd been hoarding and adding to for over a month.

A few MREs.

Water was the most critical item they carried, and it constituted the bulk of the weight in their packs. Running out of water would be a sure death sentence. Cade was not going to let that happen.

Liam had a similar stock of food and water as well as a twenty-foot length of rope, a hatchet, work gloves, extra ammo for his rifle, and duct tape.

"Seriously?" Harper reached for the duct tape and held it up. "This is important enough to include in your bug-out bag?"

"Sure. You'd be surprised how many times a bit of duct tape can save the day."

The tension between Harper and Liam had fallen away in the last ten miles. Cade suspected it simply required too much energy to remain angry. And honestly, what did he or Harper have to be angry about? That Liam had followed them? If he hadn't...

Cade shut his eyes, blocked out that thought, focused on a mythical place in the mountains that could offer them a fresh start.

When he opened his eyes, Harper was reaching for the bag of jerky. She pulled out a piece and tossed the bag to Liam who did the same then passed it to Cade.

Liam resumed the conversation they had begun the day before. "I asked Tía where you were going, but she acted like she didn't know. Kind of surprised me, since she always seemed to know everything else."

"We were headed north," Cade explained. "Lincoln National Forest—Cloudcroft."

Liam hooked a thumb back the direction they'd come. "You missed your turn-off."

Harper laughed. "Yup. We're in foreign territory for certain."

"Tía insisted that we go east—head into Guadalupe National Park, hole up in McKittrick Canyon if we have to. She was pretty adamant about it."

"She has a convincing way about her." Liam studied his piece of jerky then tugged off another bite.

Cade was thinking that a guy Liam's size would need a minimum of 3,000 calories a day. The beef jerky wasn't going to do much for him.

Liam washed down the bite of jerky with a measured sip of water. "I get why you decided to leave. In fact, I remember you standing up at the last council meeting and suggesting the camp be moved in stages."

"He certainly tried, but they didn't go for it." Harper stuffed her two extra sets of clothes into her pack and used it for a pillow, lying back and staring up at the sky that was a stark, cloudless blue.

Liam fidgeted with his roll of duct tape. "Why the secrecy about leaving?"

"We couldn't afford to let it become something people were going to vote on. We're aware that I'm the only doctor in the camp, but I did my best to train three other people in the last few weeks."

"It won't be enough," Liam pointed out.

"You're right. It won't. But in the end, Harper and I decided that we needed to do what was best for us." Cade sent him a pointed look. "And you need to do what's best for you...regardless of what Tía said."

"Says the man who changed his destination based on that same woman's suggestion."

"It was a bit stronger than a suggestion." Harper continued staring up at the sky.

Cade glanced up, thought he saw sunlight reflecting off something. Too small for a plane. A drone? He hadn't seen one of those in over a month. Whatever it was winked out, and he wondered if he'd imagined it.

He turned his attention back to Liam. "We appreciate your covering us back there. But you need to think about this. Going to a supposed new community is one thing, heading off into the desert with no clear destination in mind is another. After all, we don't plan on living at Guadalupe. I'm not sure that's any more sustainable than the barrio."

Harper's voice held no criticism when she said, "And yet that's where we're going."

"Tía told me to take the trail to the top—that I would be able to see..."

"What? The future?" Liam laughed and took another small drink from his bottle of water.

"I don't know what, exactly. She told me to do it, so I'm going to. I trust her...instincts."

"Call it what you want, that woman freaks me out a little." Liam began stuffing items back into his pack. "But I trust her too, and that's saying a lot these days."

Harper sat up and gazed directly at Liam. "So you're going with us? All the way to Guadalupe?"

"Yes. At the pace we walked today, we should be there in..."

"Six, maybe seven days." Exhaustion washed over Cade like a wave that he was powerless to stand against. "We'll climb the trail to the peak, see what there is to see, and assess our options."

"Sounds like a plan that I'm down for."

They spent the rest of the day resting, cleaning their weapons, packing and repacking their supplies. When the sun sank beneath the western horizon, Liam stood, shouldered his pack and picked up his rifle.

Those actions told Cade that Liam understood just how precarious their situation was.

Never leave your pack.

Your pack is your survival.

Keep it with you at all times. Keep your firearm in your hand or very close to it. Keep alert and be ready to move.

"I'll take first watch." Liam nodded at them and walked into the deepening darkness. He would walk a quarter mile perimeter for the next two hours and since he was taking the first shift, he'd also take the last. That left him the intervening four hours to sleep.

Four hours.

Too few calories.

They couldn't do this for long, but they could do it for five days. Maybe that would be enough.

Cade lay down next to Harper, rolled toward her, and placed his hand on her stomach. He could feel her smile, and then she put her hand on top of his.

This was real.

His hand, her hand, and beneath those their baby.

Whenever he doubted what he was doing—and he definitely did have his moments of doubt—he thought of their child and the path seemed...if not clear, at least discernible.

"You've changed," she said.

"Have I?"

She traced a finger over the back of his hand. "When I met you..."

"More than three months ago."

"Your hands were still soft." She flipped his hand over, traced the scars on his palm. "Unscarred."

"I had doctor's hands before. A doctor tends to protect his hands at all cost. We think that we heal with our hands." He propped himself up on his elbow so he could study her in the last bit of light. "You've changed too."

"I have?" Her eyes opened. She studied him, but she didn't smile. She waited.

"Sure. That young woman who walked up to the west fence..." He shook his head, laughing silently. "You brought your laptop."

"Yes, well I was going to need my laptop if I was going to make my next deadline."

"Took you a few weeks to realize your schedule had been cleared—permanently."

"I was trying to hold on to the past." She raised up enough to kiss him on the lips—gently, softly, and then she flopped back down.

"It's more than that," he said, his tone suddenly serious. "It's as if this thing we're going through has chiseled away the superfluous parts."

Darkness had fallen completely.

He couldn't see her watching him, but he could feel her gaze. His words caught in his throat because they were true and tragic and beautiful. "What's left is solid and good and essential. You're a miracle, Harper Moore."

"You might be overstating your case, Cade Dawson."

He kissed her hand, held back the other thing he wanted to say so she would fall asleep—so she and the baby would rest.

But he was thinking about a quote by Michelangelo. Something about seeing the angel in the marble and carving until he set it free.

He knew that Harper wasn't an angel, but she was special. And this thing that they were going through? It would either carve away the shell and set them free or it would be the end of them.

Chapter 5

L IAM STEPPED OFF A quarter mile from the campsite and then proceeded to walk the perimeter at a slow and methodical pace. At first he could hear the low murmur of Cade and Harper talking. That died away and still he waited. When he guessed it had been an hour, when he was as sure as he could be that they were asleep, he dropped his pack on the ground and reached into the concealed pocket sewn in the side lining.

He pulled out the device he'd been issued and powered it on. His thumbs poised over the small keyboard. Then he began to type.

Headed east with the target.
Following route quarter mile north of Highway 62.
Harper, Dawson and myself.
Intermediate destination GMNP.

He hit send, watched for the indication that the message had been delivered, then waited for a reply. He didn't have to wait long.

Will intercept at GMNP.
Notify when you are 24 hours out.

He powered down the device and stuck it back in the concealed pocket of his pack. Then he picked up his rifle and resumed his patrol.

Chapter 6

H ARPER WOKE TO THE low murmur of Cade and Liam talking. She sat up, stretched, then walked fifty yards away and squatted behind a yucca plant, careful to watch for snakes, centipedes, and scorpions as she did so.

By the time she returned, Cade had created a small fire and was boiling water. He had explained his methodology to her on one of their first overnight scavenging escapades. There had been a half a dozen folks in that group. The night before she had moved into the bus with him.

Their romance had been swift.

It had felt like destiny.

It still did.

"No fires at night because they can be seen a long way off. In the morning, it's less likely that we'd be spotted, so you at least have hot coffee to look forward to."

Many things had changed since then, worsened actually. But Cade's cautious, disciplined ways remained the same.

Soon Cade, Harper, and Liam each clutched a mug of instant coffee as they tried to slowly consume their half cup of GORP—Good Ol' Raisins and Peanuts. They'd added a portion of their daily ration to the stash for the last month. The resulting mix they'd created included raisins and peanuts as well as a few chocolate pieces, some Chex mix, and bits of dried apricots. The stuff was pure protein and sugar—exactly what they needed.

The question of the day was whether they should risk diverting south to look for supplies in the small unincorporated community they'd spotted the night before. It was why they'd stopped early, but Cade insisted they weigh the risks versus benefits as a group.

"Anyone see any lights?" Harper asked. She'd patrolled after Liam and before Cade. "I didn't see a thing."

"Nothing," Cade said.

"If there were any cook fires, I would have expected to see them this morning." Liam shook his head. "Best I could tell, the area south of here is deserted."

"So do we skirt around the perimeter or walk through the center of it?"

"Anything on the perimeter will have already been scavenged," Cade reasoned. "We could use more supplies. We have enough to make it to the mountains, but we have no idea if there will be anything there once we arrive."

"First rule of scavenging—" Liam grinned.

"Take what you find, when you find it." Harper had learned that lesson the hard way the first time she'd gone out on a scavenger run. She'd come across a case of apple juice. She could clearly envision the smiles on the children of the barrio when she came back sporting it. But it was early in the day, and she didn't want to cart that case around with her for the next six hours.

So she left it.

And on the return trip, when she hurried into the old convenience store to fetch it, the case was gone. All that was left was a clean square on a dirty floor.

They hadn't seen another person on that entire trip, but someone had been travelling behind them—someone not in the barrio. Which gave rise to the second rule of scavenging.

Never assume you're alone.

"How do we do it?" she asked.

Liam deferred to Cade, which surprised her. Liam had always seemed like a guy with strong opinions. She'd thought he might be more assertive, but he wasn't acting that way now.

Cade nodded south. "We leave one person on the highway to stand as look-out."

Harper raised a hand. "Let me guess. That's my job."

Cade laughed. "You're good with a Sig, plus Liam and I could probably carry more out. Assuming there's anything to be had."

Harper knew what he was saying made sense, but she didn't like it. She didn't want to be separated from Cade, and she wanted to see what was in those neighborhoods.

"I'd rather go in with you."

Cade looked as if he were about to mount a solid argument, but Liam shrugged. "Let's go in together, then. I don't see how it can be a trap, but if anyone's headed in toward us, we'll hear them in plenty of time to mount a defense."

They were packed up and heading east in twenty minutes. The sun hadn't yet risen, but the sky was light. It occurred to Harper that the desert was beautiful in its own way.

If it didn't sting, poison, or starve you.

If you had water.

They stopped to the north of the small cluster of buildings, with Highway 62 between them and whatever they were about to encounter.

No cars moving.

No people walking.

No sound at all.

"Let's do this," Cade muttered, then led the way across the highway and down Loma Linda Boulevard.

Harper kept twenty feet behind Cade, and Liam maintained the same distance behind her. Harper's hands were in her pockets, palms wrapped around the grip of her handguns, ready if she needed to use them.

The bulk of the town, if that's what you wanted to call it, was to the southeast—nine streets deep, six streets wide. There were houses and convenience stores, a grocery, a feed store, a small school, a church.

But there were no people.

Most of the shelves in the convenience store and grocery store were empty, but whoever had done the looting hadn't bothered with the feed store. They found a virtual treasure trove there—candy bars and packages of jerky and a cooler that was no longer cold but was filled with bottles of water and pop.

Liam searched behind the counter, found a duffel bag, and they proceeded to fill it.

There was a small area of clothing, and Harper walked over to see if she could find anything useful. Most of it was the wrong size, though she did snag them each two more pairs of hiking socks. That was a real score. Her hands froze, though, as she looked to the right where a small display held baby clothing. There were onesies—a blue one with a picture of a John Deer tractor on front and a pink one with horses. She took one of each, folded them carefully, unzipped her pack, and set them on top.

Harper wasn't sure exactly how she felt about the new life growing within her. She sometimes questioned the wisdom of bringing a baby into the world they now inhabited.

Some days, it didn't even seem real.

She'd gained no weight and had no morning sickness, but the other symptoms were all there.

A missed period.

Fatigue during the first few weeks.

Sensitive breasts.

When she'd told Cade, he hadn't been surprised. Some days, she forgot he was a doctor. He'd found some pregnancy tests in one of his scavenger runs, and they'd easily confirmed it. They'd calculated that she was eight weeks along.

That was the day they began planning to leave the barrio. It had been a good place to regroup in the first few months after *the fall*, but it wasn't where either of them wanted to raise a child.

As she walked to the front of the store, she saw Cade put a dozen packets of seed into his pack—tomato and onion, carrots, green beans, sunflowers. He zipped it up, then grinned at her as he wound his arms back through the straps. "Never know when we're going to want to stop and plant some things."

It had been a running joke between them, a relentless dream.

They could become farmers.

Learn to raise animals.

Begin again.

Liam now carried his rifle with one hand and the tote with the other. If it was heavy, he gave no indication.

They were on the way out of town when Harper noticed a flash of color to her right. She stopped, stared in that direction, then saw it again. A blanket with bold stripes. As she moved closer she saw that it was wrapped around the shoulders of an old man.

He didn't speak, didn't wave a hand as they approached, but his eyes assessed them.

"Howdy," Cade offered.

The old man nodded.

"You here by yourself?" Liam asked.

"I am."

Harper squatted in front of him. "Where did everyone go?"

"Away." His hand—aged, wrinkled, brown—came up, and he pointed to the north, the west, the south.

"My name is Harper. These are my friends, Cade and Liam."

"I am called Cochiece."

"Why are you here alone?"

"I said I was here by myself, and yet, I am not alone. My people are all around me."

"Your people?"

"My grandfather was of the Mescalero Apache Tribe. My grandmother was white."

Harper glanced at Cade then Liam. Cade joined her, squatting in front of the old man. Liam remained standing, his eyes surveying the buildings, the road, the mountains, then back again.

"Where did the town people go?" Cade asked.

"When the thing happened which happened, some waited but many drove away." Cochiece smiled, revealing a gap between two front teeth, his eyes becoming mere slits. "Many were afraid when the power did not come back on.

They thought that since the small screens no longer glowed, that the sun and sky and rain would also disappear."

Harper and Cade exchanged looks, but Cochiece didn't seem to notice.

"And yet, the sun continues to shine. The sky remains. The rain..." Now he pointed to the south.

Harper couldn't see much in that direction. Maybe more mountains. Maybe some clouds. Certainly nothing to be concerned about.

"The rain will come again soon."

"Cochiece, we are headed east." Cade removed his pack and sat it on the ground, then he sat in facing the old man, mirroring his posture. "Did any of the people from this town go that direction?"

"No. They thought the mountains to the north would save them, or the city to the west. Some even said that the one safe place would be the border to the south." He raised his right hand, closed his fingers into a fist, and tapped his heart. "The fear they carried with them no doubt slowed their journey."

"And the ones who stayed. What happened to them?"

"Many trucks came. Tan. The color of the desert. Long like the serpent. The men with rifles loaded those who had stayed into the trucks. Promised them food and medicine and safety." His expression turned troubled.

Troubled and sorrowful.

"They lied."

"What do you mean?"

"Perhaps they had food, even medicine, but they took the people for another reason." He pulled the blanket more tightly around his shoulders, though the morning was already growing warm.

Harper stood, walked over to Liam, unzipped the duffel bag, and removed three of the bottles of water and two of the candy bars. She took them back to Cochiece and placed them on the ground in front of him.

"You are kind," he said. "Thank you."

"You're welcome. We're sorry that we can't stay."

"There is no need to stay with this old man. I am not afraid, and it is peaceful now."

She didn't know how to answer that, so she cinched up her own pack, thought of the baby onesies inside it, and looked again to the south.

Were those clouds?

Were they building?

"Try to reach shelter before the storm arrives," Cochiece warned. "Find a safe place and wait there. Wait for it to pass. Only then should you continue on your journey."

Harper didn't know what else to say. She didn't know what else to do. She didn't want to leave this old man, but neither could they take him with them. And he seemed content in a way that Harper couldn't fathom.

She glanced back once, glimpsed the bold stripes of the blanket that had first caught her attention.

They saw no other person as they left, weaving their way among the remaining houses and stores. After they'd once again crossed the highway and resumed their trek east, Cade took the duffle from Liam and carried it for a few miles. They continued that way, alternating who carried the extra supplies, until they reached the border patrol station, where they stopped for their midday rest.

Chapter 7

C ADE PUZZLED OVER WHAT the old man had said as they made their way
toward the border patrol station. The tan trucks Cochiece mentioned
were probably military vehicles.

Why would they load people into them?

Where were they relocating the people to?

What could possibly justify that sort of action?

They'd seen nothing of this sort in the barrio. Was it because they were armed
and gated? But a military convoy could have rolled through their perimeter fence
with no problem at all. Unless it had been to their advantage not to do so.

None of it made any sense.

He pushed the problem out of his mind as they approached the border patrol
station. The small building was set to the south of the highway. In actuality they
were more than a hundred miles from the border, but the station was set up to
intercept and inspect vehicles that might be carrying drugs or people.

White letters on a green sign read simply *Inspection Station*. Below that and
affixed to the same pole was a smaller sign, this time black letters against a white
background that read *Please Dim Lights*. There were two lanes in each direction
on this portion of Highway 62. The northbound lanes could be closed, diverting
motorists to the station and requiring them to wait in a single file line.

A large metal roof over the exiting lane and the station provided some relief
from the desert sun. The station itself couldn't have been larger than a convenience store. Flying on a pole in front of it was the U.S. flag. Cade stopped,
staring at the flag flapping in the breeze.

Stars and stripes.

Land of the free.

Home of the brave.

His eyes stung with unshed tears, his heart knock-knock-knocked against his ribs, and his stomach rocked with dread at all they had lost and all they might still lose.

How many times had he sung those words at a baseball game?

How many times had he hurried by a flag, never pausing to consider its history or its future?

Something twisted deep within himself as he faced the fact that the country he'd grown up in might no longer exist. It was easy to forget that in the day-to-day struggle for survival. Facing the flag though, it brought home the reality of their situation.

"You okay?" Harper placed a hand on his arm.

He looked up in surprise, saw that Harper and Liam were studying him.

"Yeah. I'm good. It's just that…well, I haven't had much time to wonder about the state of the nation."

"Hard to do when you're fighting to stay alive," Harper murmured.

Liam simply nodded in understanding.

The station was empty.

There was coffee, sugar, and cream stored in the cupboards, which they added to their supply duffel. Those simple things were a real find. Any other day, it would have been a cause for celebration. But the old man and the deserted station had combined to set Cade's teeth on edge. He wanted nothing more than to put this place behind them.

"They must have switched to a manual log when the grid went down." Harper was running her fingers along a ledger that had been left open on a desktop. "It says here that on June 6th they switched to back-up power via the generators."

Cade sank into a chair and studied her as Liam continued to look through cupboards and drawers. Something was bothering him like an itch between his shoulder blades. He couldn't put his finger on the problem.

Hell, what wasn't a problem?

But this was something else. Something he should be able to see. Something that hovered on the edge of his vision, but as soon as he turned his head it was gone.

Harper was still hovering over the ledger. "On June 8th, they were called to assist at the border and this station was closed."

"No surprise there, I guess."

"Yeah, but look at this..." Harper picked up the ledger and brought it over to Cade, placed it on the counter in front of him. She pointed to a note penned to the right of the June 8th entry. "Orders from Major General Sean Bernabe. Unable to confirm with DHS."

Harper looked at Cade.

Cade looked at Liam.

Liam shrugged. "Comms were down everywhere, so it would be difficult to confirm."

"Yes, but..." Harper stared up at the ceiling for a moment. "I did some research for a book a few years ago. The main character was a border guard. All border patrol stations are under the supervision of the Department of Homeland Security—that's what the DHS means in this note."

"They couldn't confirm the orders they received from Ft. Bliss—orders to abandon their station and assist at the border." Cade sighed. "I don't know what it means."

Liam seemed unperturbed and unsurprised. "It means that when something happens the magnitude of what happened on June 6th, things go FUBAR very quickly."

Cade stood. "I think we should move on."

"Move on?" Harper looked surprised.

"Yeah. It's just a feeling I have—like we're sitting ducks. We should go."

"You'd rather be out there?" Liam nodded toward the desert. "In the middle of the day?"

"Yeah. I would. Plus if the old man was correct, there's a big storm coming. I'm thinking we should push on."

"How far do we have to go?"

Cade could picture the map in his head. He didn't like what he saw. "Seventy-three miles."

"Wow. So four and a half more days, maybe five."

"Yeah. We'll need to pick up our pace."

Liam looked as if he wanted to argue, but in the end he did what Liam typically did. He shrugged, nodded, and said, "Think I'll visit the head first." He walked to the back of the office and through the door marked *Restroom*.

Harper held back, a look of concern covering her face.

Cade took the rare moment alone to stand and pull her into his arms. "It's probably nothing. Can you keep going? Are you feeling okay?"

"I feel fine. I just...I don't like when plans change. You were planning on taking our mid-day break here. Right?"

"I was, but now." He kissed the top of her head, closed his eyes and breathed in the scent and steadiness of her. "I think we should go."

He'd learned to listen to his instincts when he'd done a rotation in the emergency room, and those instincts had only grown stronger since *the fall*. He didn't want to spend a moment longer than necessary in this station.

The next five hours were grueling as they walked under the midday sun. The only thing that made it possible was the southerly wind which cooled the sweat on their bodies, crystallizing it into a thin layer of salt. When they spotted a rest area to the north of the road, they all agreed it would be a good place to rest and refuel.

The rest area was one of the more modern ones put up in recent years by the State of Texas. Shaded picnic tables dotted the area next to the parking lot. The doors to the visitor center were unlocked. The building itself was modern with tall ceilings, a plethora of display maps and large bathrooms.

Harper excused herself and headed to the ladies' room. There was no running water, but there was at least a bit of privacy, toilets (that might or might not flush, depending on whether there was any water), and mirrors. The skylights allowed the afternoon sun to splash across the tile floors.

Cade walked around the room, studying the maps, looking for anything that he might have missed, that he might not have thought of yet.

"How far along is she?" Liam was sitting on one of the benches, elbows on his knees, hands interlaced. He was staring at the floor and waiting.

Cade didn't ask how he'd known. "Eight weeks."

Liam nodded. "I suppose that makes sense and goes a long way to explaining why you decided to leave the barrio."

"Yeah."

"Do you have a plan once we reach the national park?"

"I do not."

Liam swiped a hand over his face. "Are you familiar with the area?"

"I am."

"Not a lot out here, boss."

Cade shook his head at the word *boss*. In charge was the last thing he wanted to be. "Maybe we'll have a better idea once we hike to the top of Guadalupe Peak."

"And what do you suppose you're going to see?"

"He'll see whatever Tía wanted him to see." Harper clomped across the lobby, sat on the floor, and proceeded to stretch her hamstrings and calves.

"You a yogi or something?" Liam teased.

"Something."

Cade stared up at the sunlight coming through the skylights. "We've made a good pace since leaving the barrio. How about we make camp in this building tonight?"

Harper and Liam both looked at him in surprise.

"I know, that doesn't sound like something I would say."

"Does sound like what you said earlier today." Liam leaned toward Harper and lowered his voice. "Maybe he's suffering from heat stroke."

"Maybe an alien has replaced the Cade we know and love."

"You're both wrong. I've been craving one of those MREs the last three miles. We can set up our cookstove in here and no one will see it." Cade dropped his pack and headed to the men's room. "Dibs on the chili."

"You can have that chili," Harper called after him. "I've been daydreaming about the hash brown potatoes with bacon."

Cade stripped down in the bathroom and used a precious amount of his water to wet a washcloth and clean off as best he could. Then he changed into a fresh set of clothes. Stepping closer to the mirror, he searched his reflection.

He didn't mind the gray hair.

He didn't even mind the wrinkles that had appeared overnight.

But staring at his reflection he couldn't deny that something had rattled him earlier. What had happened back at the border patrol station? Why had he felt so sure it wasn't safe there? And why did he feel differently here?

Maybe he was tired.

Maybe he was seeing threats where there weren't any. Which also meant he could be missing the ones that were bearing down on them. He finger combed his hair, wet his toothbrush and cleaned his teeth.

Yup.

He almost felt human again.

A hot meal would go a long way toward making things right. Protein and carbs could change a man's perspective. Add in twenty liters of water and the woman he loved, and he would feel ready to tackle the final sixty miles.

Liam's question tagged along behind him as he repacked his things. Did he have a plan? He'd had one, but it was becoming less likely with each mile they walked east.

He retraced his steps to the lobby and rejoined his group. Cade knew he would climb the trail to the peak of Guadalupe Mountain. He'd do it because he'd promised Tía that he would. But in all honestly, he had no idea what he expected to see.

And he had no idea what they'd do after that.

Questions for tomorrow.

For tonight, he had a gourmet meal to rustle up.

Chapter 8

L IAM AGAIN TOOK THE first patrol. Eight p.m. to eleven-thirty. Harper would take the middle three hours, and Cade would cover from the end of Harper's shift until daybreak.

Though Harper and Cade were tucked away inside the rest area, Liam still waited until he was out of sight of the front or back doors before pulling out his device.

He'd sent the last message from the bathroom at the border station. Now, when he turned the device on, his message was still the last thing on the screen.

Back your drone off. He's getting nervous.

There had been no reply, but there'd also been no drone following them from the border station to the rest area.

None that he could detect, anyway.

It had been a stupid move by his superiors and unnecessary. He was updating them regularly. If Cade were to begin to suspect Liam's motives were compro mised...

Honestly, he didn't know what would happen.

He didn't think Cade would shoot him. The man was a doctor. He was hesitant to resort to violence, but he would to protect Harper. To protect Harper and his child, Liam corrected himself.

A twinge of guilt caused him to look up and away. He'd had no trouble with the assignment when it was only Cade they were after. Seeing Harper by his side, seeing the way they looked at each other—looked out for each other—made things a bit harder on his conscious.

But a job was a job.

He had taken a vow, and he would remain true to it.

He would push through.

Realizing that she was pregnant had complicated things in his mind though. The right and wrong of what he was doing had reared its ugly head. Which was simply another way of saying what he'd told Cade and Harper earlier.

Things go FUBAR very quickly.

It had certainly happened to him before. Why should this assignment be any different?

Refocusing on the device in his hand, he keyed in their location and reiterated for those in charge to keep the drones away from them. The response was immediate.

Will intercept at GMNP. Confirm when you are in place.

He read the message twice, then powered down the device.

Unfortunately, he had three hours to kill, walking a perimeter, watching for lights or cars or any sign of other people—all things he was very adept at doing. What he wasn't good at was turning off his brain.

His mind insisted on replaying what the old man had said.

Many trucks came... men with rifles loaded those who stayed...promised them food and medicine and safety... they took the people for another reason.

If what Cochiece had said was true, Liam understood what it meant. The government was rounding up people on a large scale.

Not what he had been told.

But, he had only been told what his superior deemed he needed to know. He could connect the dots though. It wasn't that hard, and now he realized that he just might have connected them incorrectly. He might have drawn what he wanted to see. If what Cochiece had described had happened in the way he'd described it, what he had done and what he was doing was wrong, immoral, unacceptable.

No.

There had to be another explanation. Perhaps the old man was confused or mis-remembering. Maybe he'd jumped to conclusions that, in the end, would prove incorrect.

Liam didn't like it. He would follow orders—to a point. He wasn't exactly sure where that point was, but he'd know it when he reached it. And what the old man described came dangerously close.

Chapter 9

H ARPER SLEPT BETTER THAN she had the night before. There was something about being inside, whether it was in the old bus they'd used for shelter over the last three months or a roadside rest stop.

She felt safer.

She realized that might be an illusion.

Being inside also meant that they could be trapped if anyone attacked. But she trusted Cade. She even trusted Liam, though she still didn't understand why he'd chosen to leave with them. Why hadn't he gone on to Cloudcroft? Why had he, like them, followed Tía's instructions?

It took them nearly four more days to cross the remaining sixty-five miles of desert from the rest area to the Guadalupe Mountain National Park camping area. They simply could not maintain the pace of the first few days. Several times Harper had leg cramps, and they had to stop while she rested and hydrated. Cade constantly readjusted the pack on his shoulders, and Liam grew even quieter than his normally reticent self.

They had decided not to detour to Dell City, a small crossroads to the north that basically consisted of a motel on both sides of the freeway. The Guadalupe Mountains that rose before them started as a smudge on the horizon and loomed larger with every hour. When they stopped at the scenic overlook, El Capitán, still several miles distant, seemed to loom over them. They dropped their packs onto the ground and stared up at the giant rock face.

"Southernmost promontory of the Guadalupe Mountains," Cade explained.

Harper rummaged in her pack for another water bottle. "Spanish for captain."

"Correct."

"Sign says we're three miles from the campgrounds." Liam had his eyes on the road, not the mountains.

They gave El Capitán one last glance, then trudged on.

Harper had never been in this area. She'd traveled to Dallas, Houston, and San Antonio. Always by air. And she'd grown up in Albuquerque. The move to El Paso had been for a job.

One that didn't work out.

One that pushed her into attempting what she'd always wanted to do.

Write.

"How do you know so much about the area?" she asked Cade.

"Hiked it with my dad. He thought everything worth seeing was in Texas. We hiked either Big Bend or Guadalupe every year." Cade shook his head as if the memories were laughable.

They'd talked about their parents.

Wondered how they were.

Had Cade's father survived? He had recently turned sixty, as had his mother. Had they opted to stay in Houston or tried to evacuate? Harper's parents had always lived in Albuquerque. They loved visiting the mountains to the north, but would they have gone there to stay? Would they have been able to find transportation?

Since both of their families lived in large metropolitan areas, they'd decided any search for them would have to wait. Finding a safe place to live, especially now with the baby, was their primary objective.

Their only objective.

Cade nodded toward the mountains. "Guadalupe Peak is the highest point in Texas. It's elevation is nearly nine thousand feet."

"The mountains look so rugged."

"They are. Salt flats and desert dominate the west side of the park."

"The part we're walking through." She'd finally grown used to how barren everything looked.

"Exactly. On the east side there's grassland."

"When there's rain," Liam interjected.

"And within the interior of the park are canyons and alpine uplands. It's a pretty varied ecosystem."

"What are the canyons like?"

"Beautiful in the fall. McKittrick in particular is amazing. There are natural springs, trees, even some old cabins."

Harper held that picture in her mind. A cabin next to a spring. A place tucked away in the mountains.

Liam ruined her daydream when he said, "Wouldn't want to get caught in a canyon during a storm though. The water comes down fast and rises quickly." He nodded to the bank of clouds building in the south, then resumed his normal silence.

It was past noon when they reached the national park. Cochiece's predicted storm had lowered the temperature and brought a strong wind. Harper wanted to hike to the peak that afternoon. To finish what they'd promised Tía so they could move on to what they needed to do.

Cade and Liam vetoed that idea.

"Don't want to be on a mountaintop during lightning."

"Don't want to come down those switchbacks in the rain."

Sometimes their carefulness was enough to drive her to complete distraction, but she understood that they were right. Harper realized in that moment that her uneasiness had been growing since the moment they left the barrio. She needed to be headed in a direction away from this place. She needed to be headed toward their future, not gazing into their past.

But she had no idea what that meant.

They found that the Pine Springs Campground had been abandoned.

"I'm not sure I expected to find people, but I certainly didn't imagine this." Cade stood in the middle of a row of camping sites, hands on his hips, turning in a circle.

Tents and RVs had been abandoned in their spots. Food and supplies and towing vehicles had been left behind. So where were the people?

A few times Harper felt an intuitive warning creep up her spine. Was someone watching them? She never saw anyone. Never even heard anyone.

She was tired.

She was pregnant.

And her imagination was operating in hyper-drive.

They had initially passed the visitors' center with only a cursory look. It was obvious that the place was abandoned. Now they retraced their steps, entered through the front door, and stood gazing at the open space.

There was no food in the gift shop. "Probably taken by the campers," Liam offered.

"Yeah, but then where did the campers go?" Cade was once again standing in front of a giant wall map. "There are a lot of trails...quite a few even cross into New Mexico."

Liam walked over and stood beside him. He studied the map a moment, then turned and looked out the window. "You've got two kinds of campers, in my opinion. Retired folks, who are here for the scenery and the easy hikes."

"They didn't hike to New Mexico," Cade agreed.

"Then where are they?" Harper had hauled herself up onto the counter top at the visitor center booth. She was sitting there, swigging water and swinging her feet. She felt a little guilty sitting on the counter, as if a park employee would show up and admonish her. But she didn't feel bad enough to stand up again.

"Good question."

"The other kind of hiker is your young kids—I'm talking twenty-something. They're here for the challenge."

"Where are they?" Harper repeated.

"And why didn't either of those groups take their stuff?" Cade shook his head. "We can bed down in here or in one of the campers. Ride out the storm, then hit the trail tomorrow morning."

"According to Cochiece, it's going to be a big one." Harper craned her neck to the left to better be able to see the gathering storm through the front glass doors. Though it was only late afternoon, the sky had taken on an otherworldly darkness. "Looks like it could get pretty hairy."

Liam lowered his pack to the floor. "This space provides more exits than an RV, should we need them."

"Agreed." Cade ran a hand through his hair. "Harper, you want to search the offices, see if you can find any information?"

"Sure."

"Check drawers and cabinets for any food or drink." Cade turned to Liam. "Could you do a quick run-through of the campers and tent sites? Look for any type of critical supplies. No need to drag it all over here. We'll gather and pack supplies after we hike to the peak. Make a note of anything we might need in the next month."

The next month? They'd only been on the road a week, and Harper was exhausted. She had no idea where she'd find the strength to continue for another month. In that moment, she felt more tired than she could ever remember feeling. More tired even than when she'd first shown up outside the barrio's fence. It was a deep, bone-weary, muscle-aching, all the way to her soul tiredness.

Maybe it was the baby.

She couldn't tell, looking at her stomach, that she was even pregnant. But the profound weariness suggested that the pregnancy was taking a bigger toll on her than she wanted to admit.

Cade must have noticed the dismay on her face. "I don't know where we're going next, but I do know we can't maintain the pace we've set since leaving the barrio. That means we're going to need more supplies because wherever we're going and however we're getting there, it's going to take some time."

"On it, boss." Liam grinned and headed back out the entrance. A gust of wind caused the door to slap shut behind him.

"I guess I'm kind of glad he came along," Harper admitted.

"Have I told you lately that you're amazing?" Cade walked over to her, put a hand on each side of where she was sitting and leaned in to kiss her lips—once, then again. Pulling back, he grinned at her. "You are a hiker extraordinaire."

"I think the fact that you took me along on your scavenger missions helped get me in shape."

"That was the idea."

She reached for him then, put her arms around him and pulled him close, breathed into his neck and smelled the sweat, kissed him and tasted the salt on his skin.

"Yikes. Get that started and Liam will come back to a scene he does not want to see."

Harper grinned. "Maybe we can find a private place to bed down tonight."

"Maybe we can."

It was one of the lightest moments they'd shared, and Harper wished it could last. It didn't. Lightning streaked across the sky and thunder crashed. They were in for a hell of a storm, but at least they would be inside when it hit.

Liam came back with additional food he'd found in the camping sites. He pulled a piece of paper out of his pocket and handed it to Cade. "I also made a rough map of what campsites have things we might want to take with us. I don't know what happened here, but I don't like it."

"What did you see?" Cade had done a perimeter sweep of the visitor's center, making sure there were multiple unblocked exits out, but only one way in. Unless the person attacking had an RP-G, in which case they could blast through a wall.

"They left everything." Liam sank into one of the plastic chairs that Harper had brought out into the open area near the front doors. "Guns, ammo, food, clothing. I don't know where they went, but I can tell you that they did not plan on going there."

Harper was sorting through the cans of food that Liam had returned with. "Could you tell how long they'd been here? What I mean is—"

"Were they here since the beginning, since June 6th? Maybe. Some of them. Their stores of food seemed to be more depleted. But some of these people had lots of food and lots of water. That indicates to me that they'd just arrived here. And one person..." He walked over to his pack and rummaged through an outer zipper, pulling out an eight-inch by six-inch journal with a rubber band that acted as an elastic closure. He opened the journal and paged through it.

"The name written in the front is Aubrey. Probably a teenager. She's big on exclamation points. Aubrey seemed to be documenting what happened." He flipped through the pages to two weeks earlier, then turned it so that Cade and Harper could read what was there.

September 19—I didn't want to come out here, didn't want to leave all my friends, but honestly most of them had moved on already. Dallas was like a movie set for a zombie movie. Well, there weren't zombies but people were acting like there were. We saw someone shot and left on the side of the road outside our neighborhood. When the house next door was ransacked, my parents packed us up and took off west.

A guy my dad used to teach with said there was a community in New Mexico, but honestly I think they were just needing to put some miles between them and what used to be home.

SEPTEMBER 20—I don't know if I can handle this. There's nothing out here. Nothing!!! No stores. No hospitals if Tommy has an asthma attack. And what are we going to do when our food runs out?

SEPTEMBER 23—There are a lot of tent campers and folks in RVs here.

I met a guy named Dwain. He's two years older than me and acts even older than that. Dwain says there haven't been any park rangers here for a really long time. He also says he'll teach me how to shoot.

SEPTEMBER 24—at night we "circle up." That's what they call it. Everyone gets together at what used to be an amphitheater. We don't watch movies. People share what they've found to eat, or where they've found water. If anyone has seen a car pass out on Highway 62 they describe that too.

SEPTEMBER 25—Some military people came in jeeps. They said that the government is clearing out this place. They'll be back in two days and everyone should be ready to go. My mom wants to leave before they return. She doesn't trust them. But where would we go?

SEPTEMBER 26—They didn't wait two days. They came back at day-

break. Dwain's dad argued with
them, said they couldn't make him
or his family go. They shot him in
the back and just left him there. My
hand is shaking so bad, I can barely
write.

Harper smoothed the page with her fingertips. The next few lines were smeared with Aubrey's tears. How old was she? Fifteen? Sixteen? And where was she now?

Is this really happening? I can't be-
lieve it's really happening. I can't stop
crying and Mom says we have to go
now...If I take this, they'll probably
just destroy it. I'll take my other jour-
nal and leave this. Maybe someone
will read it. If anyone does, remember
you only have three choices: go with
these assholes, run, or hide. Mom's
saying—

The ink slid off the page in a haphazard line.

Harper sank into another of the plastic chairs, suddenly nauseous and trembling and unsure if her feet would hold her. "It's just like what we heard from Cochiece."

Cade had taken the journal from her and was leafing back through the pages. "Maybe there's a resettlement program we don't know about."

"Sure. Except the term resettlement usually refers to a voluntary program." Harper put her head between her knees.

Why was this journal from a girl she didn't know affecting her so much?

What was she afraid was going to happen?

She put a hand to her stomach and focused on quieting her mind, on breathing deeply and evenly, on doing the things she had learned through her meditation app in what seemed like another lifetime.

"Anyone who doesn't want to go gets a bullet in the back." Liam's voice was hard, teetering on the verge of anger. "This is not what our military is supposed to do. This is just...I need a minute."

He snatched up his hat and strode out the doors.

Harper looked up in surprise as Liam stormed from the room. She heard the sound of the wind and the first splatter of rain. She lowered her head again and didn't realize that Cade had taken a seat beside her until she felt his hand rubbing circles on her back.

She pulled in one deep breath, then another. Finally she sat up straight and looked him in the eyes. "I thought I was ready for whatever we might find."

"Yeah, me too."

"I wasn't ready for this."

He nodded, the worry in his eyes mirroring what she felt.

She attempted to put some resolve in her voice. "What do we do?"

"Put out whatever containers we can find. Catch enough water to have a good wash. We'll feel better when we're clean and rested."

"And tomorrow?"

"Tomorrow we hike to the peak. We see whatever it was Tía wanted us to see, and then we get the hell out of here."

Harper felt immediately better. The hiking was hard. Not fully understanding their situation was hard. Being hungry and tired and dirty was hard. But knowing they had options? That made those things bearable. They didn't have to stay here. They didn't have to stay on this road that seemed to be a trap waiting to snare them.

She didn't know what was going on with the military or their government—if those two things even still existed. But she knew she could trust Cade. She knew she was a strong woman, and that she would be able to do whatever she needed to do. And she knew that with Cade and Liam on her team they would find a way out of this.

All of the good people in the world hadn't disappeared. They would find them, and when they did they would also find the place they were going to raise their child.

Chapter 10

T HE RAIN BEGAN LATE that afternoon and lasted until a few minutes before nine that evening. The storm finally slipped past them, but it had packed quite a punch. Cade suspected some of the tents they'd seen were now in the next county.

On the plus side, they'd captured enough rain water for everyone to clean up and even wash their hair. That, plus the full dinner they'd had, mitigated some of the uneasiness he'd felt on reading the journal.

It was plain that someone was rounding up people and forcing them onto transports.

Why?

Where were they taken?

Who was doing it?

Cade didn't have any of those answers. It bothered him, but it didn't bother him enough to keep him awake. As soon as he slid into the sleeping bag Harper had spread out on the director's couch, as soon as he wrapped his arms around her, he was asleep.

They maintained a watch, the same way they had every other night. Liam took the first shift, as had been his routine. Cade wanted to let Harper sleep through her shift, but she'd set the alarm on her watch. It was an old Timex they'd found on one of the scavenger trips. The thing had to be wound each day to keep ticking, which Harper meticulously did.

She was up before Liam even came inside.

He reminded her to be careful and immediately fell back into a deep sleep. It seemed like he had just closed his eyes when suddenly Harper was snuggling up beside him. "Your shift, Romeo."

That didn't seem possible.

He'd slept another four hours?

He snagged his hiking pants, boots, and pack, and tried to sneak out of the room. He needn't have worried. Harper's soft snores reached him as he carefully shut the office door.

Liam was passed out in the gift shop, which at least had carpet on the floor. He didn't move as Cade made his way through the lobby.

Stepping outside, Cade looked up at a star-filled sky. The rising moon gave just enough light to allow him to see the outline of the mountains. He was glad they hadn't attempted the hike the afternoon before, or worse yet, continued on to the canyon. He wouldn't have wanted to be crouched under a rock ledge as the water came sluicing down toward the desert floor.

He walked the route they'd predetermined—behind the visitor center, through the Pine Springs Campground, out to the road, then back to the visitor center. He heard nothing other than the night birds and the occasional howl of a coyote. He saw nothing except the stars, the outlines of the building, tents, and RVs. His mind slipped back to the journal. He couldn't help picturing all the people in their RVs, in their tents, forming a community and thinking that possibly they were safe.

Until the unimaginable had happened.

How was it that they so often could not imagine a situation growing worse? It was as if something in the human psyche said *this we can deal with, but after this things will improve.*

Only they didn't improve, not always.

Not in this case.

He thought of Harper and the child growing inside her.

He pictured Liam and found he was grateful the man had followed them.

Cade could imagine an ever-worsening cycle of events if he bent his mind to it, but he wouldn't. There lay the way of madness.

He woke the others when the eastern sky lightened ever so slightly. By daybreak they were at the trailhead to Guadalupe Peak. He'd made the suggestion to Harper that she might want to sit this one out.

"Is that your recommendation as my doctor?"

"No."

"That's what I thought." She cinched up the straps on her pack. "Thank you, but I'd rather tag along."

Liam was trying not to laugh. It was plain enough that Harper was a strong, independent woman, but Cade had thought convincing her to hang back was worth a try.

Though normally they kept all of their items on their person, they decided to leave most of their extra food supplies and water at the visitor center. They'd found a ring of keys in the director's office and used them to lock the door of an equipment closet where they stuffed their supplies. The lock could be broken, of course, but if someone was passing through and in a hurry, they wouldn't take the time. They'd grab the food and water Liam had found, which he'd placed on a round visitor center table, and scamper away.

"The trail is 8.4 miles round trip, with an elevation gain of 3,000 feet. The toughest section is the first mile, which includes a lot of switchbacks." Cade waited for Liam and Harper to indicate they understood what he'd said. When they did, he smiled and said, "Let's do this."

He'd always enjoyed hiking with his father.

It had always invigorated him.

Reminded him of his place in the grand scheme of things.

Cade went first with Harper right behind him and Liam bringing up the rear. The land unfolded around them as darkness gave way to daylight. The Chihuahuan desert was a place of dazzling beauty when viewed from the trail. It didn't look nearly as rugged and deadly as it in fact was. Cade understood the reality versus the illusion, but he still found his mood lifting as they hiked up and away from the mysteries of the campground behind them.

The previous day's rain actually made the trail less crumbly.

"I saw someone almost slide over the edge once," he said to Harper when the trail had widened enough for them to walk side by side.

"Seriously?"

"Dad and I were hiking down. A group of three women were in front of us on the switchbacks. They were moving a little too quickly." He shook his head at the memory of his fear. "In an instant their hike went from pleasant to terrifying."

"What happened?"

"The person in the lead lost her footing, fell on her butt, and began to slide. The second person reached out and grabbed the leader's backpack, hoping to slow her descent."

"Did it work?"

"Nope. Instead, she, too, had been pulled off her feet. The third person in the group had grabbed the second person's pack and managed to stop the slide."

"Wow."

"Yeah. I stood behind them, my mouth open, eyes wide, afraid I was about to see my first hiking fatality. Once the group of three backed away from the edge, they had a hearty laugh about it, but it was plain by the way their hands shook that it had been a close thing."

He didn't realize Liam had been listening until he said, "A close call like that is a real wake-up call. I've seen it before. People get complacent, until they nearly die."

Cade took it as a good sign that they were once again a group of three. Like those hikers so many years ago, he knew that Harper had his back, and Liam had hers.

Where the trail intersected with the one going back down to Devil's Hall, they stopped to catch their breath and hydrate. The second mile was still steep, with areas of stone steps, but it was definitely easier than that first mile.

"Yikes." Harper stepped carefully closer to the wall of the mountain and slowed her steps a bit. The trail had indeed narrowed, one side dropping away dramatically.

"Hang in there, darling. The bridge is coming."

At just over three miles they passed a sign pointing to the Guadalupe Peak Backcountry Campground, which was situated on a ridge to the right. They continued on for the final mile of trail enjoying the panoramic views of both the park and the rugged country beyond.

The bridge was in fact an old wooden affair that spanned a crevice in the trail. It had been there as long as Cade could remember, certainly since he was a young teen and had hiked with his father. He could vividly remember sitting on the bridge and tossing pebbles down into the gorge.

Harper wasn't interested in sitting on the bridge.

He could practically see the muscle in her jaw flexing as she gritted her teeth and made her way cautiously across.

Catching him watching, she stuck out her tongue, then laughed and said, "Bet you thought I'd panic."

"I did not."

"Panicking is not allowed," Liam chimed in.

They scrambled up the last bit of trail, over rocks, and to the summit. The area around the summit was large enough for them all to spread out, and in the middle was a monument.

"Strange," Harper said, hands on her knees, attempting to catch her breath. "I wasn't expecting a metal pyramid thing."

"Why does it say Post Office Department?" Liam asked.

"Because it commemorates the 100-year anniversary of the Butterfield Overland stagecoach, which passes to the south of here. The three logos are—"

Harper had moved closer to the monument and was peering at the words. "American Airlines, USPS, and Boy Scouts. Ha. If only they could see us now."

The view was incredible and gave the impression that if you looked hard enough you might be able to see into tomorrow. Or yesterday. The thought slipped through Cade's mind that maybe if they looked long enough, they would see their own past. Perhaps they could see the beginning of this thing they were caught up in, the exact moment it had begun. Maybe they'd see why it had begun.

El Capitán was now below them. The day was picture-perfect with only a few fluffy clouds drifting across the sky. A light breeze cooled their skin. Cade had once hiked the trail in the afternoon when the winds were high. He didn't think Harper would appreciate the views then. She'd probably ask for a parachute just in case she was blown over the edge.

They each pulled out a protein bar and their bottles of water. He was raising his bottle, anticipating the cold relief of the liquid on his throat, when he thought he saw the morning sun reflect off something in the distance. He slowly drank the water, keeping his focus on the thing. He suspected if he looked away, he would lose it.

"Harper, mind fetching the binoculars out of my bag?"

"It's sitting at your feet."

"Yeah, I'm aware." He was leaning forward now, peering into the distance, trying to locate some type of landmark, but the land looked the same left to right, near and far.

Harper had scooted next to him, retrieved the binoculars, and placed them in his hands. He was conscious of Liam turning from what he was looking at and peering instead in the same direction Cade was looking.

He raised the binoculars, adjusted the focus and shook his head. It must be a mirage. It couldn't be...

"What? What are you seeing, Cade?"

"I don't..." It couldn't be what it looked like, but then the light shifted again and all doubts fled.

Hundreds upon hundreds, maybe thousands of tents the color of the desert seemed to stretch to the horizon. And maybe it was that small change of the light again, but he could suddenly make out jeeps, buses, even people moving about.

They had found an encampment.

But it wasn't the new community in Cloudcroft.

This was from the old world, and he had a feeling that a great majority of the people scuttling between tents weren't there because they wanted to be. They'd been loaded onto buses and forced into this camp.

There was no fence around the tents, but there didn't need to be. Anyone who fled would either be shot by one of the guards he could now make out, or they would die in the desert. With no supplies and from that location, they wouldn't last more than a few hours.

The people below weren't going anywhere except where they were told to go.

This wasn't a resettlement camp.

It wasn't an evacuation camp.

The people he was studying had been imprisoned.

Chapter 11

T HEY REMAINED AT THE summit another twenty minutes, passing the binoculars back and forth, watching the people below, trying to make sense of what they were seeing.

Harper felt suddenly nauseous, and it had nothing to do with her pregnancy. It was sheer, stark fear.

What exactly were they up against?

What did this mean for their plans?

Where would they be safe?

She closed her eyes, took three deep breaths, then opened her eyes and focused on Cade. "Is this what Tía wanted us to see?"

"Yes. I don't know how she knew about it. I don't know how she knew we'd see it from here, but...yes. It has to be."

Liam was silent. The expression on his face seemed to be chiseled from stone. His eyes gave no clue as to what he was thinking.

The trip back down the trail should have been easier, but they were weighed down with the knowledge of what lay to the north. Harper felt as if her pack was twice as heavy. There was no bantering about fear of heights. In fact, they didn't speak at all as they crossed the wooden bridge and continued down.

Liam led the way down, Harper was in the middle, and Cade brought up the rear. She gradually became aware that she couldn't hear his footsteps behind her. Turning, she saw him standing in the middle of the trail, hands on hips, staring down at the ground. When he raised his eyes to look at her, she felt a cold chill pass through her bones. She actually shivered, though the day was growing warm. Her granny would say that someone had walked over her grave.

"Liam." When he turned, Harper motioned back toward where Cade was waiting. They retraced their steps, stopped, took in what he was staring at.

"But..."

"How..."

Cade shook his head, pressed a finger to his lips. The footprints were small. Surely they belonged to a child. Cade motioned toward the side trail that led to the backcountry campground. Walking side by side, they moved down it, came around a bend, and saw the single tent.

There wasn't much else in the camp area.

There wasn't anything else.

Someone had made a small stack of wood next to the fire ring, but there was no smoke rising from it. As they stood there in the middle of the trail, watching, they could make out two shadows in the tent, elongated by the sun passing through the tent walls. It was impossible to tell the sex or even the age of the two people.

Cade motioned for Liam to circle to the other side and for Harper to stay on the trail, then he approached the tent. When he was within ten feet, he called out.

"Hello?"

The two shadows that she could make out inside the tent froze.

"My name is Cade...Dr. Cade Dawson. We were hiking down the trail and saw your tent. Are you okay? Do you need any help?"

There was the low murmur of voices, what sounded like a boy arguing with someone. Then a small girl poked her head through the tent flap, and a boy pulled her back. He placed his body between her and Cade.

His action provoked an ache in Harper.

That children, a boy no more than ten, would feel the need to protect his sister from a stranger caused her to press her palm against her chest. That the world had come to such a state was nearly more than she could accept.

"Are you really a doctor?" The boy eyed Cade suspiciously, glanced at Harper, then turned his attention back to Cade.

"Yes, I am. Is your mom in the tent?"

He nodded once, a quick short yes.

"Is she sick?"

The boy nodded again. He was a slight child with blonde hair that fell into his eyes. He raised a very dirty hand up to brush it away. His face and clothes were also covered with dirt, and his shoes—the shoeprint they'd seen at the juncture of the two trails—were caked with mud.

Cade dropped his pack on the ground and raised his hands, palms out. "Looks like you're taking good care of your sister. Would it be okay if I came in and looked at your mom? Maybe I can help."

Harper thought he would say no. She thought that the fear in this boy's heart would win out over the desperation in his eyes. It didn't.

The boy drew himself up to his full height. "Do you have a gun?"

"There's one in my pack. I'll leave it here on the ground. I'm not going to hurt you. I wouldn't do that."

The boy shook his head once, disbelieving.

"What's your name?"

"Jack."

"Jack, this is my wife, Harper."

She offered a small wave.

"And over there is my friend. His name is Liam."

The boy glanced in Liam's direction. He seemed to realize he was surrounded. His expression changed from defensive to worried. "Why are you here?"

"Because we promised a friend that we'd hike the trail. She wanted us to see something at the top."

"The camp?"

"Yeah. The camp."

"So you're not with them?"

"The soldiers?" Cade shook his head. "No. We're not with them."

"My mom, she's bleeding. And now she's hot."

Cade nodded toward his bag. "Is it okay if I get my medical kit out of there?"

Jack stared at it a moment, then said, "Okay."

Cade pulled out the medical bag he'd packed near the top and made his way into the tent. The boy's attention was split between his mom, his sister, and trying to keep an eye on Harper and Liam.

Harper took the smallest step forward. "Liam and I are going to sit near your fire ring. Okay?"

"I guess."

Liam took a circuitous route, but eventually joined her. "Looks like they're alone up here," he said in a low voice.

They could hear Cade speaking to the woman, his tone soft and professional. At one point the little girl peeked out at them, then ducked back inside. She was smaller than the boy. Younger, though just as dirty.

"What's your sister's name?"

"Olivia."

It took no more than ten minutes, then Cade appeared in the doorway of the tent. "Can your sister sit with your mom while we talk?"

"Yeah. That's what she does when I go down for supplies."

"Makes sense." Cade nodded approvingly. "You two have done a good job caring for your mom."

Jack didn't speak, but he pulled in his bottom lip when it began to quiver. Finally, he pushed out his fear in the form of a question. "She's not going to get better, is she?"

"Let's sit."

Jack spoke to his sister, who disappeared back in the tent. Harper could hear her sing-song voice as she spoke to her mom.

Harper, Liam, and Cade sat on one side of the fire ring, the side with their back to the tent. Jack sat across from them. His eyes continually scanned the tent, the ground, then the group in front of him.

"What happened, Jack? Who shot your mom?"

"One of the soldiers." His voice was flat, resigned. "She didn't want to go with them. When they came early in the morning, when they came before they were supposed to, she told us to run. She said she'd meet us on the trail."

"That must have been frightening."

Jack glanced back toward Cade and nodded. "Everyone was crying and hollering, then one of the soldiers fired his gun up in the sky. Everybody got real quiet after that. They were scared so they got on the buses."

"But not your mom?"

"No. I guess she thought they wouldn't notice her. She tried to sneak out the back side of the campground, but they saw her."

Liam's voice was hard, flat. "And they just shot her? She was unarmed and they just shot her?"

"Yeah." Jack had picked up a stick and was raking it across the ground, back and forth, back and forth, in a mesmerizing rhythm. "I guess they thought she was dead. I saw her from the trail, and she saw me, but she shook her head. She wanted me to wait, so I did. Is that why she's dying?"

"Your mom was shot in the back. The bullet didn't come out the other side. I suspect she lost a lot of blood at first."

"When they left, she had me wrap her up. First with Saran wrap and then with a strip of sheet."

"You did a good job, Jack. That your mom was able to walk up the trail after that? It's because you did such a good job."

Jack shook his head, tears streaming down his face. "But not good enough, right?"

"I can't be sure without an x-ray. I think the bullet missed her spine but punctured her intestines, and that led to gastrointestinal fluid leaking into her abdominal cavity. That's why her stomach is so swollen. You didn't do anything wrong, Jack. It's a hard wound to survive, even if you're in a hospital."

The boy stood, his shoulders bowed as if he were carrying the weight of the world, and Harper supposed he was. Certainly he was carrying the weight of his world.

Without another word, he walked into the tent.

Harper, Cade, and Liam sat in silence, and then they began putting together what must have happened. The family of three had hid, waited until the soldiers left, retrieved their tent, and finally made it up the trail.

"Where's the father?" Harper asked.

"Ashley—the mom—told me he was killed while they were still in Dallas. He was trying to get some food from a grocery store, and someone shot him. That's why she brought the kids out here. Fight, flight or freeze. She chose to flee. They had experience camping, and she thought they'd be safe here."

"Did she confirm what the kid said? About the soldiers?"

"Pretty much. As you can imagine, she doesn't have a lot of strength, but what she said fits with what Jack told us."

"And with the journal Liam found."

Liam stared at the ground.

"How long does she have?" Harper asked.

"Less than twenty-four hours. I'm surprised she's lasted this long."

"So we stay with them and then..."

"And then we take the kids with us." Cade didn't even hesitate.

Harper loved that about him. He didn't waiver from doing the right thing, even when it added to his burden.

"There's barely any food in the tent," Cade said. "Between what we have in our packs, I think there's enough to feed the kids and ourselves for a day at least."

They set about building a campfire, encouraging the kids to eat, taking turns sitting with Ashley. The day passed slowly. Harper learned that Jack was ten years old and had been in Cub Scouts. Olivia was only six, and although at first she was afraid of them, exhaustion won out. After she'd eaten a bowl of oatmeal with raisins, she fell asleep, clutching an old, worn doll.

Harper and Cade took turns sitting beside Ashley, bathing her face with a wet rag, offering her sips of water, which she took less and less of. Cade had given her some morphine to help with the pain. Twice while Harper was sitting with her, she woke—a look of panic in her eyes as she searched for her children.

"They're okay, Ashley. Jack and Olivia are okay."

The woman didn't speak. She no longer had the strength for that. This wasn't one of the scenes Harper would have written in a romance novel. There were no death bed confessions or pleas.

How did you describe the agony in her eyes without words?

How did you put so much suffering on a page?

Harper realized that she had known very little about life when she'd been a writer. She had thought she could describe living and dying and all that lay in between while observing it from a distance, but that wasn't really possible. And now that she had experienced so much loss? So much compassion? She wasn't sure she had the courage to write those things down.

"We'll take care of them," she whispered. "I give you my word that we will."

What happened next was like something in a novel. Ashley sighed deeply, nodded once, and then closed her eyes. The westerly slant of the sun cast a glow across the campground, bathing the tent in a soft light as if to bless her passing.

Chapter 12

I T DIDN'T TAKE LONG to pack up the few supplies the children had. Cade said a few words over the woman, though they weren't able to bury her. They were on a mountain top. The ground was basically rock.

Liam had left men behind before.

No soldier wanted to do that and yet twice in his deployments it had been necessary. He understood the need to bury, to protect the body of your brother, your sister, your mother. He looked at Jack, and he knew now was the time to make a decision.

He also knew what his decision had to be.

He turned to Cade and Harper. "I need to talk to you both. Privately."

Cade had been about to shoulder his pack. He looked up in surprise. "Now?"

"Yeah. Now."

Harper glanced at the kids. Liam did the same. Jack was trying to distract Olivia, showing her the makings of a bird nest in a tree that had begun to lose its leaves. Jack glanced up, sensing that the adults were hesitant to leave them alone. "We'll wait here."

They walked far enough away to not be heard, but still close enough to see the kids. Liam couldn't think of any way to cushion his words, and he didn't think they had time for such luxury. "You can't go down the trail."

"What do you mean?" Cade was completely focused on Liam now, as was Harper.

"A group of soldiers are waiting in the campsite—waiting to take you both."

"I don't understand." Harper's eyes widened.

Liam knew Harper was a strong woman. The last week had confirmed that, but he suspected she had experienced too many highs and lows in the last twenty-four-hour period. She seemed to hear what he was saying, but her expression suggested his words were not getting through. Cade, too, looked confused. Distracted even.

Instead of answering, Liam dropped his pack, reached into the concealed pocket and pulled out his comm unit. He powered it on, then offered it to Cade, who held it so that Harper could see the words that appeared on the screen.

From Cpl. William Contreras
Sent 30 SEP
"Back your drone off. He's getting nervous."
"Will intercept at GMNP. Confirm when you are in place."

~~~~~~~~~~

From Sgt. Lester Tompkins
Sent 04 OCT 23
"We are in place. Intercept tomorrow."
"Location?"
"Pine Springs Campground."
"Make it afternoon."
"Copy."

Both Cade and Harper seemed too surprised to respond. It had been almost four months since either of them had seen words on a digital screen. They stared at it, trying to make sense of the messages. Harper pressed her fingertips to her lips, glanced at him, then back down at the screen.

Cade was the first to recover.

He pushed the device back in Liam's hands, as if it were covered in poison, as if he couldn't get rid of it fast enough. He pointed back toward Guadalupe Peak, to the tragedy unfolding in the desert beyond.

His voice, when he found it, was a growl. "You're with *them*?"

"The soldiers guarding the tents? I know nothing about that."

"Well, you're providing information to someone."

"It's my job, Cade. My assignment—"

He didn't get any farther. Cade slugged him in the jaw, causing him to stumble backwards. The pain was instant, blinding, deserved. Cade must have put every ounce of frustration and fear and anger into that punch. He might not have stopped there, but Liam made no move to protect himself. Hands lowered to his side, eyes pinned on Cade, he simply waited.

Hell, part of him understood that he had earned the punch and more. But another part of him knew that if he couldn't get through to them, right now, they didn't stand a chance against what was waiting in the campground at the bottom of the mountain.

Chapter 13

CADE STARED DOWN AT Liam, holding the man's shirt in his left hand, his right pulled back to hit him again. The red haze that had colored his vision dissipated, and he dropped Liam in the dirt. Walking away, he faced the opposite direction, took in three deep breaths, and told himself the emotions would have to wait.

He pivoted back toward the two people he'd set on this course with. The two people he had depended on.

Harper was more true than true north. One look at her told him that she had understood what the messages meant. Her eyes were on the children. Cade's eyes went to her stomach, to his child, and finally back to Liam.

"Why are you telling us now?"

"Because I didn't know about what's in the desert there past Guadalupe Peak, okay? All I knew was that my commander tasked me with identifying and recruiting high value assets."

Cade covered the distance between them in three long strides. "Recruiting? Don't you mean kidnapping?"

"Because you wouldn't have wanted to go? Because you'd rather spend your skills as a physician laboring in some third world camp rather than helping to put this country back together?"

"As if you care what this country—"

Harper pushed her way between them. One hand on each of their chests, she gave them both a shove—a surprisingly strong shove.

"Stop it," she hissed. "Those kids have been through enough today."

Her words were like a splash of cold water on a fevered brow. Cade reined in his emotions, put them in the proverbial box, and slammed the lid shut. "How long do we have?"

"They'll wait until dark, then they'll come looking."

"But they're in position already?"

"I imagine so, yes."

Cade dropped his pack to the ground, pulled out the trail map he'd picked up at the visitor center, then walked over to a boulder and spread it out on top. "Show me."

"Their plan is to intercept here, at the Pine Springs Campground. They'll have the exit blocked."

"Can you send them a message?"

"Yes."

"Are they tracking us?"

"Yes."

"With that?" He nodded to the device Liam was still holding.

"Yes."

Cade used a finger to retrace their route down the mountain, came to the intersection of Devil's Hall and tapped it. "Send a message. Say that we saw the desert camp. Say we had second thoughts and changed plans. Say we're headed this direction, down Devil's Hall Trail."

"They'll know it isn't true."

"They won't, because you're taking that device with you. You're going down Devil's Hall. They'll follow you in, and while they're doing that, we can escape."

"Even if they believe that, even if they follow me into Devil's Hall, they'll leave men and their vehicles at the campground. You won't be able to get past them, and you certainly can't outrun them on foot."

"We'll take one of the vehicles left by the campers." Harper had been standing several feet away, listening and watching the children. Now she pushed her way in between them. "The vehicles will still work, right?"

"They should." Liam stared at her. "What are you thinking?"

"That if you can distract them long enough..." She leaned forward, traced Devil's Hall over to Tejas Trail, and beyond, far beyond, to McKittrick Canyon. "Don't tell them we saw the camp. Just say that we are tired, don't know where else to go, and are headed for the cabin in McKittrick Canyon."

Liam rubbed fingertips across his brow. "It might work."

"They'll pull their men and vehicles. They'll take the main road northeast..." She tapped the map. "To the trailhead for McKittrick. If you can make them believe it, that would be their best move. From there they'll beat us to the canyon."

"They'll beat us to the cabin," Cade said, understanding and agreeing.

"If Cade is an important enough asset." Harper raised her head slowly, fixed Liam with her stare, with those intense green eyes that Cade knew so well.

"He is."

"Then they'll pull out and track him."

Liam nodded.

"So you'll do it?"

"Yes." Liam didn't even hesitate, and Cade gave him points for that.

"What happens to you then...when they realize it was all a ruse?"

"I hope to never find out." He shouldered his pack. "Stop at the top of the switchbacks. If they believe the story, you'll see their vehicles leaving, headed toward McKittrick. There will be three army vehicles. Make sure all three leave before you descend the trail."

"Okay." Cade had moved past his anger. He needed to conserve all of his energy. He needed to get Harper, Olivia, and Jack to a safe place.

"What about you, Liam?" Harper put a hand on his arm. "Can you double back? Lose the device, destroy it or toss it into a ravine part of the way down Devil's Hall, then meet us in the campground?"

Liam glanced at the map.

He seemed to be calculating the mileage in his head.

Cade knew that covering that much ground in that short a time period wouldn't be easy, but then he wouldn't be slowed down with the kids. Also, he was in the military. He'd probably been receiving extra rations on the sly.

"I'll try. Watch for the three ISVs to leave."

"We don't know what that is."

"Infantry Squad Vehicles. Can carry nine men. Like a jeep on steroids." Liam waited for Cade and Harper to nod that they understood. "Wait for the ISVs to leave. Then pick a vehicle, siphon gas out of the other vehicles, have everything packed and ready, including our extra food. If I'm not there by ten, leave without me."

He turned and headed down the trail at a fast clip, waving at Olivia and Jack as he passed them.

Cade reached for Harper, waited until she'd turned those green eyes on him.

"Why?" His voice was soft, low, and filled with all of the questions that he had. As much as he loved Harper, he realized that he still didn't completely understand her. Maybe he never would.

"Why what?"

"Why do you care what happens to him? Why would you trust him to go with us?"

She stepped into the circle of his arms, rested there a moment, and then pulled back so that she could look at him directly.

"Liam didn't have to tell us, and he was as horrified as we were by the tent city, by what Jack told us. I was watching him. I watch people. That's how I write, how I was able to write." She ran her fingertips down his jawline. "I read people, Cade. Liam did not know the government was forcing civilians on to transports."

"Okay."

"People change, Cade. People can change."

"Maybe."

"There's another reason though."

She stepped away, picked up the map, handed it to him. He folded it and stuck it into his pack.

Harper's voice was gentle, calm, and certain. "Tía wanted him with us. Why else would she have told him to follow us?"

The old woman wasn't a soothsayer or a prophet. She wasn't infallible. But she also hadn't led them wrong yet. What Harper said, it made sense. Cade didn't know if he trusted Liam or not, but he did know that in a strange twist of fate Liam had again saved their lives. This time, he'd saved them from a future that they neither wanted nor had even known was waiting for them.

Liam had thrown his lot in with them.

Cade supposed the least they could do was give him a second chance.

Plus, Liam knew things...things that Cade thought would be valuable to them and whatever community they finally joined. One thing that was becoming increasingly clear to him was that they didn't stand a chance doing this alone. They had to find a group, a solid group, and work with them if they hoped to survive.

They hiked the rest of the trail slowly, partly because Jack and Olivia were tired. Cade doubted they'd slept much in the previous days as their mother's condition had worsened. But they also moved slowly because they needed to reach the start of the switchbacks as darkness faded to night. They had to be in position to watch and confirm that the military vehicles had left.

They would need to time this just right.

"How many trips have you made to the campground, Jack?"

"A few."

"That was a brave thing to do."

"Can't really get lost unless you turn at Devil's Hall, and I knew not to do that."

"No trouble with the weather?"

"A couple of times, before dark, the wind came up. That was kinda scary."

"I've been on this trail when it's windy, and scary is right. The last time it happened to me I was a teenager, and I was terrified."

Jack seemed to assess him, as if wondering whether Cade was simply placating him. The boy had a sharp mind and a strong survival instinct. The question was whether he'd decide they were trustworthy. At the moment, he didn't have any other options, so he was going along with what they said. Cade wouldn't be surprised if he decided to run. He wouldn't go without his sister though, and at the moment, she was bonding with Harper.

"Can I get my dolls?" Oliva asked. "I left all but this one in the camper. We had to run."

"We'll get your dolls, for sure."

"I have two more." She proceeded to skip along the trail, telling Harper about her playthings. Twice Harper reached out and pulled her back when she danced too close to the edge of a drop off. She finally settled for putting her body on the outside of the trail and asking Olivia to walk on the inside.

They walked slowly, hydrated often, and reached the beginning of the switch backs as the sky was fading from deep blue to black. As Jack had described, the wind increased, but it wasn't one of those days where you were afraid of being swept off the mountain. It was more a gentle wind, enough to cool the sweat on your brow.

Cade led them around the corner of the first switchback, then motioned for everyone to sit on the trail with their backs up against the dirt slope. Olivia sat as close to Harper as possible, and the next time Cade looked the little girl had her head in Harper's lap, her eyes closed.

Jack was wide awake. He was taking his responsibility to look over his sister seriously, much too seriously for a ten-year-old. Then again, it was what the situation had demanded.

"Will they be able to see us?" Jack asked. He kept his voice low, barely above a whisper.

Cade looked at Harper, Olivia, Jack and finally down at himself. "We're pretty dirty, pretty much the same color as everything else here. I don't think they'll see us." He pulled out his binoculars, focused them on the camping area, and easily found the three military vehicles. They were easy to pick out.

Like a jeep on steroids.

The ISVs were lined up across the entry, and Cade counted four men and two women, all wearing military fatigues.

He handed the binoculars to Jack, who looked surprised, then accepted them. His face hardened as he studied the vehicles and the people.

"Are they the ones that killed your mom?"

"No. The guy who did that was really tall and had black hair. I don't see him."

Jack passed the binoculars to Harper. She stared down at the ISVs and Army personnel, then scanned the campground. She handed them back to Jack and nodded toward the far side of the camping area. "See the Jeep Wrangler Sport? I think it's our next ride."

Jack nodded in agreement, though he muttered, "Not a lot of space."

"We don't plan on living in it." Cade accepted the binoculars and focused on the jeep with oversized wheels. "Good choice, Harper. We could go off road, if we needed to."

"Probably gets good gas mileage too."

Which brought up the question of where exactly they were going. Cade didn't know. One look at Harper told him she didn't know. It was something that they'd need to decide at some point, and soon. He was about to bring it up when one of the men beside the ISV pulled a device out of his pocket and stared at it.

"Liam sent the message." His words came out as the barest of whispers, as if now they were in more danger of being seen or heard than they had been seconds before.

The man staring at the device showed it to someone else, then began shouting orders that they could hear from their spot on the trail. "We're moving out. The target has redirected to..." The wind picked up and Cade missed the next few words, which were followed by an emphatic, "Now."

First one ISV then the other peeled out onto the road. The last remained in the parking area. Cade felt a sinking dread in the pit of his stomach. Had the guy in charge told the last group to stay back? Were they covering their bases? It was what he would do.

Finally, the engine of the third ISV roared to life. With a punch of the accelerator it jumped forward, then sped down the road in fast pursuit of the others.

Chapter 14

T HEY BASICALLY TUMBLED DOWN the trail. In the years that followed Harper would look back on that day and those moments as a watershed. Before it, she had held on to the hope that life might one day return to normal. Discovering the tent city beyond Guadalupe Peak, hearing Jack tell of what had happened to his mother, and sitting with Ashley as she died changed Harper's conception of the future.

Holding Olivia in her arms.

Witnessing Cade's passionate anger.

Seeing Liam's expression of soul-crushing regret.

It all combined to bring a stoic realization and acceptance to Harper's soul. The life she had known was over. There would be no going back.

This moment and these people were all she had. And it would be enough. She vowed to make sure that it was enough. She would not lie down or give up. She would not look away. She couldn't afford to do any of those things. She had to fully accept the reality of their situation for herself and for Cade and for their baby. For Jack and Olivia.

They descended the trail in forty minutes. Jack took Olivia to their camper for extra clothes and a few personal items. "Don't forget her dolls," Harper whispered.

Jack nodded, then took his sister's hand and hurried in the opposite direction.

Cade headed for the jeep.

Harper went to the visitor center to gather the supplies they'd hidden in the closet. She found a push cart dolly, loaded their supplies on it, then maneuvered it out into the night. There were no lights operating throughout the camping complex, except for the stars. She was growing used to navigating by starlight.

By the time she reached the jeep, Cade had set out two small lanterns on the ground. They provided just enough light to work by. He'd apparently found the keys to the jeep and was cutting what looked like an IV tube into two sections—one smaller, one larger.

"Sure we won't need that for a medical emergency?"

"We don't stand much chance of even having a medical emergency unless we get out of here." His voice was low and relaxed as he took a strip of sheeting, tied the two sections of hose together, and put one end of both sections into the gas tank of an adjacent pick-up truck.

"I read about how to do this once on Google."

"Ahh, the days of Google."

"It was for a book I was writing—" She stopped midsentence. It occurred to her, standing there in the dark and waiting for the children, watching Cade attempt to siphon gas, that she might never write again.

"Actually my dad taught me how to do this," Cade said.

"He taught you how to steal gas?"

"He taught me survival skills."

Jack and Olivia arrived at that moment, both wearing backpacks that looked stuffed to the brim. Olivia was clutching all three of her dolls.

Cade glanced up at the boy. "Want to help me, Jack?"

"Sure." He waited to be sure Olivia was fine with Harper, then hurried to Cade's side. "We're stealing gas?"

"I don't think the person who owned this truck would mind."

"Probably not."

"Take the end of this longer hose and put it in that gas can...all the way down...good deal. Now just hold it and be sure that it doesn't jiggle out."

Cade pushed the bed sheet tied around the hoses flush up against the opening of the gas tank. "Ready?"

"I guess."

Leaning forward, Cade began to blow into the shorter section of IV tubing. At first nothing happened. Then Harper heard the splash of liquid into the gas can. Cade stopped blowing and pushed the pad of his thumb over the exposed end of the shorter tubing.

"It's working!" Jack stared at the can, carefully holding the tubing steady.

"Tell me when we're full."

"Nearly."

"I want you to pull it out quickly and point it up to the sky."

Jack did so, spilling only a few drops in the process. Cade took his thumb off the end of the hose.

"Harper, grab another can."

He'd found three gas cans and they were all lined up in front of the truck. She placed a second next to Jack. Gas cans and lanterns and empty trailers. There was no telling how far the occupants had travelled. She tried not to think of where they were now.

"Stick it in there?"

"Yup. Try not to spill it on your clothes."

It occurred to Harper that by involving Jack, Cade was working to restore the boy's confidence.

Cade was a good man, and he'd be a wonderful dad.

Twenty minutes later, they'd filled up the jeep's tank and placed the two extra cans of gasoline in a cargo hold in the back. It wasn't a trunk, just a small area that reminded Harper of the back of a Volkswagen beetle. It was big enough for the cans though.

The food supplies went into a cargo box that had been mounted on the back of the jeep. Their packs went on the floor at their feet. She sat up front with Cade. Jack and Olivia crawled into the back.

Her nerves felt taut.

Taut and troubled and terrifyingly fragile.

What if the military people came back? What if Liam didn't make it? What if their jeep didn't start?

The engine caught and offered a comforting rumble.

"I made sure it would turn over while you were getting our supplies," Cade explained. "Wouldn't want to put all that gas in a vehicle that couldn't take us anywhere."

He drove to the edge of the parking area. Harper thought it felt strange to be in a moving vehicle. How long had it been? Months. It had been months. Cade stopped with the jeep facing the road, ready for a quick exit, then he turned off the ignition. Harper's watch read fifteen minutes until ten p.m.

"Where are we going?" Jack asked.

"I want to go home." Olivia's voice held no quarrel. She'd simply stated a wish, one they all held in their hearts.

"Got your map?" Cade asked.

Harper pulled it from her pack and spread it out across them. Cade reached up and turned on the dome light.

Dome lights. She'd forgotten about those.

"West is out of the question."

Harper nodded her head in agreement. Though El Paso had offered a good shelter for nearly four months, she had no desire to return to the barrio.

She pulled her hair back, retrieved a hairband from her pocket, and wrapped it around three times. "North?"

He scowled at the map. "North would take us past the McKittrick Trail parking area. I'd rather not chance the possibility that our military friends left two guards at the road."

There was literally only one other road.

"South," they both said.

"But to where?" Harper traced the road with her finger. There were no intersecting roads until Van Horn.

"Once we reach Van Horn we can decide...west to the border, east to Fort Stockton, or south."

"What's south?" Jack asked from the back seat.

"Miles and miles of Texas."

Jack's voice sounded tired, weary even, but still curious. "Any towns?"

"Only a few." Cade tapped the map, met Harper's gaze.

She nodded. "It might work."

"What might work?" Jack leaned forward between the front two seats.

Harper had to fight the urge to lick a finger and tamp down his cowlick. She'd enjoyed being around the children in the barrio, but she'd always kept a part of her heart distant. She hadn't known how long they would be together.

This was different.

Jack and Olivia were with them now. They were a part of this family that they were attempting to cobble together, and her heart seemed to know and recognize that. She felt an overwhelming tenderness toward the boy who was staring intently at the map.

Cade handed it to him so that he could study it.

"Here?"

"Yes," Harper said. "Maybe. If we go south."

"Alpine. Huh. Never heard of it."

Her watch said two minutes until ten. Were they really going to leave Liam? He was the reason the military personnel had left for McKittrick. Of course, he was also the reason the military personnel had been on their trail in the first place.

Her thoughts were interrupted by the sound of someone running toward them. Cade's hand went to the ignition. Harper reached into her jacket and wrapped her hand around the gun she kept there.

"It's your friend." Jack scooted closer to Olivia, who was now sound asleep.

Liam opened the door, took off his pack and stuffed it into the floorboard, then hopped in and closed the door.

"Good to see you." Harper couldn't help smiling at this man who had very nearly betrayed them. Something told her that Liam was one of the good guys, even if he had worked for the other side.

"Good to be seen." Liam leaned forward. "I suggest driving with your lights off."

"Roger that." Caleb pulled out of the parking area, turning right on Highway 62, turning back the way they had come. He kept his speed low and his lights off. There was no one else on the road, but they'd need to watch for deer and javelina.

"Need some water?" Jack sounded suddenly wide awake.

Harper turned to see the boy handing Liam his water bottle.

"Yeah. Thanks."

He emptied it, then handed it back to Jack, who shook it and grinned.

"You looked thirsty."

For seven and a half miles, they kept their speed under forty, then they merged left and south onto Highway 54.

"Lights now?" Cade's eyes flicked up to the rearview.

"Pull over," Liam said.

When Cade had stopped in the middle of the road, Liam hopped out, pulled a pocket knife from his pocket, hustled to the back of the jeep, and raised the hatch. Harper could just see him through the back window, through the gap between the bottom of the window and the bottom of the raised hatch. Twice he reached down, found something, and pulled up on the knife.

Harper jerked each time.

Now that they were nearly away from the immediate danger, she was more on edge than she'd been before. Sitting made her nervous. Sitting in the middle of the road and wondering who could see them caused a low dread to build in her belly.

Liam quietly closed the hatch, climbed back into the jeep, and shut the door. "Taillights are disabled. The guys back at McKittrick won't see you even if they happen to look this direction."

"Do you think headlights are okay?" Cade asked.

"Low beam."

"Did you disable your comms device?"

"Pretty much."

Harper twisted in her seat. "What does that mean?"

"I passed a spring that emptied into a small creek. It had a little bit of flow, so I put the comms unit in a waterproof bag and set it adrift."

"Better than disabling."

"That was my thought."

She could see it, the small bag and the modern comms device leading the people who were pursuing them in the opposite direction.

Liam dug in his pack until he found an energy bar. "So where are we going?"

"South." Jack yawned mightily. "Some place named Alpine."

"Haven't been there in years."

"I've never been there," Harper admitted. She turned to Cade. "What about you?"

He nodded. "A time or two."

"Let me guess. You hiked there with your father."

"Actually, I did. Good guess."

She wanted to take her boots off and put her feet on the dash. She wanted to be young and carefree and relaxed. Instead, she settled into the corner of her seat, bracing her back against the door after making sure it was locked. It would be terrible to survive the walk from El Paso, the climb to Guadalupe Peak, and the flight to escape the military goons, only to fall out of a moving vehicle.

She kept her eyes on the road and her hand wrapped around the gun.

Chapter 15

L IAM SCANNED THE AREA around the vehicle continuously—left, center, right—repeat. The moon was in its third quarter, what appeared to most folks to be a half moon. Liam had been drilled on the phases of the moon, since for any type of military exercise it was as critical as the persons involved.

Planning a covert operation?

You wanted a new moon.

No light. Just you and the night.

At the moment, the moon was bright enough to allow him to see a little, but then it might also allow others to see them. He continued his surveillance checking Cade's side mirror, scanning in front of the jeep, then peering out at the desert—rinse and repeat.

Watching for anything out of place.

On alert for anything that might indicate a trap.

Prepared to intercede.

Cade and Harper were quiet, each studying the road that unfurled in front of them. It was sixty-two miles to Van Horn, and he had no idea what they'd find there. Resistance? Another empty town? Bodies? Had the military sweeps reached that far? Or was this corner of Texas so remote, so unexceptional, that it had been overlooked?

There were resources here, but not what his commanding officer was looking for.

Jogging toward Devil's Hall, Liam had tossed around all of the possible scenarios and discarded most. There were only two logical possibilities.

The first was that there was a valid explanation for what they'd seen in the desert, for what Cochiece had described, and for what he had read in the journal. They might have misinterpreted something. The information did not come from an unbiased source—in fact it came from people who were frightened, tired, and undernourished.

He didn't have a complete or accurate picture.

But sometimes when you were on an op, you had to make a decision based on incomplete information. You had to assess the situation as best you could, and you had to leave your own preconceived notions behind.

So, though he had felt sympathy when listening to Cochiece, when reading the journal, and when peering out at the tent encampment, he hadn't let that sympathy sway him from his path.

The boy's story was different. He could think of no reason to shoot an unarmed civilian who refused to follow orders. Why? Because she wouldn't board a bus?

It didn't make sense.

What if his group had intercepted Cade, and Cade had refused to go with them? Would he have been shot? That was preposterous. A dead doctor couldn't help anyone. No, they had counted on the fact that Cade would come around to understanding the situation once it was explained to him.

Not that it had been explained completely to Liam.

He'd been told that those in charge at the highest level were in desperate need of certain types of people—doctors, emergency medical personnel, nurses, engineers, police officers, fire fighters, ranchers and farmers, teachers...even writers. Cade had been a person of interest on his own. When he hooked up with Harper, they'd become doubly important to acquire.

Liam glanced at Jack, who had finally succumbed to his exhaustion.

South was good.

There were no military bases in that part of Texas.

There wasn't much of anything.

Liam needed time to piece together what he knew, the small bits of information he'd overheard from his commanding officer, and what he was seeing with his own two eyes.

He had one additional resource he hadn't dared to use yet. He hadn't shared it with Cade or Harper, hadn't allowed himself to so much as check that it was still in his pack.

It was still in his pack.

And he would use it if he needed to.

If the time came where the scenario morphed into an *Us* against *Them* situation, which nearly had been the case back at the campground, he would use it. He'd deal with the repercussions later.

The drive to Van Horn seemed to take forever, even once Liam was sure the ISVs at Guadalupe weren't following them. One threat averted. But what else waited for them in the desolate country they were passing through? And what were the chances that Alpine would be any better than El Paso?

"What can you tell us about Van Horn?" he asked Cade.

"Small town, maybe two thousand people. Depends heavily on tourism traffic—folks travelling from Guadalupe Mountain to Big Bend." Cade flicked his gaze behind them. "Still all clear?"

"Still all clear."

"Didn't I read something about Jeff Bezos buying big tracts of land in Van Horn?" Harper crossed her arms and peered out the front of the car. "Something about Blue Origin."

"Correct. Fifteen years ago Bezos started buying up land in the area, to the tune of one hundred and fifty thousand acres."

Liam seemed to remember something about that, but whatever he'd heard or read had been a lifetime ago. "For his company Blue Origin? The rocket company?"

"Exactly. We've probably passed its headquarters already. If I remember right, it was twenty miles or so north of town."

"Huh." Liam turned and looked behind him. "Didn't see a thing."

"Yeah, I don't think Jeff Bezos would have chosen to watch the fall of technology from his launch site in Van Horn, Texas."

"No doubt he has a bunker somewhere." Harper's voice sounded more amused than cynical.

"How did the people of Van Horn feel about Bezos?" Liam was thinking of small towns and hard feelings and feuds.

"As you might guess, some were for embracing Blue Origin and some weren't. One problem was that with Blue Origin personnel moving into the area, the price of houses skyrocketed. Went to nearly three hundred thousand for the median home value. Van Horn has never been what you might call affluent. Blue Origin's move into the area forced many people out."

"How do you know this stuff?" Harper asked with a yawn.

Cade laughed. "A friend of mine that worked at the hospital was from Van Horn. His parents sold out, made a good profit on the home, and moved to a retirement community in Arizona."

Silence enveloped the car as they tried to envision what Arizona was like now and how a retirement community would have fared. *Not well*, is what Liam thought. And water? Water would be a problem in Arizona. With no electricity to power the pumps, simply surviving would have become difficult fast.

When they were a few miles outside of town, Olivia began whimpering in her sleep. Jack woke, stretched, and said something to his sister.

Harper turned and stuck her head between the front seats. "Does she do that very often? Cry in her sleep?"

"She has stomach aches," Jack explained. "And she throws up now and then, especially when we're riding in a car."

Liam would have liked to move a little farther away from any projectile vomiting, but there was literally no place in the back seat of the jeep to go.

"We're almost to Van Horn," Cade said. "If it looks safe, we'll pull over."

What it looked was deserted.

They passed a café, a chain motel that had seen better days, and several deserted gas stations. From the way the glass was shattered in virtually all of the windows, Liam assumed there was nothing to be gained by stopping and searching for supplies. The word *Watchmen* had been spray-painted on several of the buildings.

"That mean anything to anyone—*Watchmen*?" Cade asked.

"Nope." Liam assumed it was a small-town gang. "Who takes the time during an apocalypse to tag buildings?"

"*Watchmen* is familiar. Maybe some kind of anarchist group?" Harper shook her head. "It'll come to me eventually."

Olivia was now fully awake. "Harper, I don't feel so good."

Harper glanced at Cade, who nodded once, took a left, and pulled into a parking area behind a hotel with an attached restaurant. Everything appeared empty and abandoned. The three adults exited the car, then all stood completely still.

Listening.

Straining to see any threat lurking at the edge of the moonlight.

Harper moved closer to Cade and Liam, then lowered her voice. "Okay to walk her around a little?"

"I think so," Cade said.

Liam nodded in agreement, then added. "Place seems deserted. Just stay close."

"Got it."

Harper walked back to the jeep and unbuckled Olivia. Jack was already out of the car, standing halfway between Harper and Cade. Glancing around, eyes scanning, arms at his side, hands clenching and unclenching. The boy was practically bouncing on his toes.

The only sounds were night sounds—birds, an owl in the distance, the wind rattling an old sign.

"What's south of town?" Liam asked.

"Interstate 10."

"Overpass?"

"Yes. The road we just came off of, Highway 54, runs under it."

"Okay." Liam reached into the back seat and retrieved his rifle, leaving the door open. He pulled his Glock from his hip holster, checked it, then holstered the firearm. "I'm going to reconnoiter. If there's a trap, that's where it'll be."

Liam jogged south, careful to maintain an eastern trajectory. He wanted to see anyone lying in wait. He didn't want to trip over them. He passed a few more Watchmen tags and what looked to be the wreckage of a shoot-out at one of the intersections. He stopped, held back, scanned the area.

He moved silently toward the car in the middle of the intersection. The front windshield was spiderwebbed from the impact of bullets. The doors had bullet holes as well. The man behind the wheel—dead. Based on the state of the body, the attack had been fairly recent. There was nothing in the passenger seat or back seat, and the trunk, which was open, revealed only empty space.

Liam moved forward with the silence of a cloud slipping across the sky. Heel to toe. Knees slightly bent. Weapon drawn.

Someone was out there. Someone was hunting, and Liam vowed that he and the group he was with would not be their next kill.

He heard two voices when he was still half a block from the bridge.

Two men.

One vehicle.

South side of the I-10 overpass.

The flare of a match gave away their position. Liam moved closer.

"Don't know why Gerald insists on us doing this every night. No one's coming this way anymore."

"You might be right, Byron, but you ain't the boss. Gerald is."

"I'll tell you what we should do. We should go ahead and hit Alpine. Anything we need? It's there."

"Maybe. Probably, even. Still doesn't make you boss."

Then Liam heard something that caused his spine to stiffen—the crackle of a radio.

"Status?"

"Status is dead, as in this place is dead."

"James thought he spotted movement several blocks north of your position. Go check it out and then report back in."

The radio clicked off, but instead of leaving, the man—Byron—lit another cigarette.

"Let's go. You heard him."

"I heard him, but that doesn't mean I have to jump when he says scat."

"He said to check it out."

"And we will, when I finish this smoke. Probably just javelinas again..."

Liam crept back the way he'd come.

He needed to warn Cade and Harper. He didn't know how many Watchmen were in Van Horn, but a good guess would be six. Liam had no doubt that this ragtag group of reprobates were the same people who had tagged the buildings in town. Depending on how the Watchmen were armed, depending on what type of firepower they carried, he and Cade and Harper could handle six men.

Or they could run.

Chapter 16

WHEN LIAM HEADED OFF into the darkness, Cade walked back to Harper and Olivia. He squatted down in front of the little girl who was already starting to feel like family.

"How are you feeling, sweetheart?"

"My tummy hurts." She turned and buried her face in Harper's jeans.

"Is it okay if I check your temperature?"

Olivia nodded and turned toward Cade. "Ahhh..." She opened her mouth wide.

"Very good, but I just want to touch your forehead."

Olivia pushed her head forward, reaching up with one hand to hold back her bangs, though she continued to clutch her dolls with the other hand.

Cool to his touch, which meant she probably simply had a case of motion sickness. "Right as rain," he said.

"Right as rain," she murmured.

"Some crackers and water might help."

"Okay. We're fine here, if you want to..." Harper nodded toward the surrounding buildings as she reached into her backpack and pulled out a package of crackers.

"You sure?"

"Absolutely." Harper patted the pockets of her jacket. "I'm armed and dangerous."

"We're both armed and dangerous," Olivia declared, then pulling Harper down to her level, she whispered, "Can I have some crackers now, please?"

"Of course." Harper opened the package, then handed it to her. "Go slow though, and take sips of water between each cracker."

"I will, Harper."

Cade turned to find Jack watching them. "Want to stay here with your sister, or go with me and take a look around?"

"You okay, Liv?"

"I'm okay." Olivia had already stuffed one of the peanut butter crackers into her mouth. Her words came out sounding like "Vime kay."

Jack turned to Cade. "Sure. Let's do it."

Cade pulled his .380 from his pack and stuffed it into his hip holster. He didn't like to wear the thing while he was driving, but he wasn't about to walk through the darkened streets of Van Horn without a weapon.

"Armed and dangerous?" Jack asked.

"Absolutely."

Olivia pushed the package of crackers back into Harper's hands. "I'm full."

"Good deal."

"Good deal," Olivia echoed.

"Let's walk around a little, honey. It'll help your tummy." Harper took Olivia's hand, and they began walking across the parking area in the opposite direction.

Cade and Jack stepped out onto the street.

More graffiti had been sprayed on adjacent buildings, including the words *Alan Moore Lives.*

"Who is Alan Moore?" Jack asked, turning on the flashlight Cade had given him and studying the words.

"I think he wrote graphic novels." Cade shook his head. "Not really my area..."

They walked past a pharmacy, and Cade said, "Let's go in here."

"Looks trashed."

"It looks that way," Cade agreed. "But it's important to follow the two rules of scavenging."

"What two rules?" Jack sounded doubtful, but he moved the beam of the flashlight slowly along the shelves.

"Hold it there." Cade walked to the end of the aisle, stooped down so that he was level with the edge of the flashlight beam, and snagged a box. He held it up for Jack so see. "Score."

"Band-aids?"

"Yup. Superhero band-aids. Might come in handy." He stuck them in his jacket pocket, and motioned Jack back out onto the street.

"So what are the rules?"

"First rule—take what you find, when you find it."

"Like the band-aids."

"Right."

Jack seemed to think about that a minute. "You're saying, don't assume you can come back and get it later."

"Exactly."

"And the second rule?"

Cade rather wished he hadn't started this conversation, but then again Jack was ten years old. He was growing up in a post-modern world, one marked by scarcity and need and danger. Jack was old enough to understand.

"The second rule is never assume you're alone."

"There might be people who want to hurt us."

"There might be."

"Or there might be people we need to help."

"Also possible."

They were back on the sidewalk now. Someone had sprayed, *Do as you please.* And across another building, *V is for Vendetta.*

"Why are you helping us? Me and Liv?" Jack asked.

"Because it's the right thing to do."

"That's it?"

"I'm afraid so. Sometimes, things are pretty simple."

"Okay." Jack was nodding now, the beam of his flashlight jiggling up and down. "I guess I can see that. The only problem is sometimes you want to help someone, but you're not really sure how."

"Like..."

"Like when I wanted to help my mom."

"Right."

"And even now. I want to help Olivia, but I don't always know how to do that. I didn't know to feed her crackers when she's carsick. I'm just a kid, Cade. There's a lot of stuff I don't know."

The misery in his voice caused Cade to stop, turn Jack toward him, and wait for the boy to raise his eyes to meet his own. "You don't have to know everything, Jack. You've done a great job, and now Harper and Liam and I are here to help."

"Okay." Jack brushed his arm across his eyes, and they resumed walking.

"And it's okay to cry. Don't feel like you have to hide that."

"Do you?"

"Do I cry?"

"Yeah."

"Absolutely."

"Like when?" Jack sounded as if he didn't believe what he was hearing, but at least he was no longer crying.

Cade thought he could tell stories all night long if it kept that note of desperation out of the boy's voice.

"I cried when I broke my arm."

"How old were you?"

"Nine—so younger than you, and for the record, it hurt like hell."

Jack laughed, a short, soft sound.

They encountered their first body a block away. Someone had been shot at point-blank range. Jack stepped closer to Cade. They moved on. Although the doors to most of the businesses had been flung open, someone had still taken the time to shatter the plate glass windows facing the streets.

When they came to the park bench where an entire family had been bound and then shot, Cade took Jack by the shoulders and turned him back toward the jeep. "Let's go. We've seen enough."

Cade pulled his .380 from the holster. He walked side by side with the boy. He suddenly realized they were too exposed. At least in the jeep, they'd had metal around them. Out here, in the dead of night, they'd be easy pickings for anyone with a thermal scope.

"Turn the flashlight off," he whispered.

Cade's spidey sense sent tendrils down his neck.

He'd assumed because the streets were deserted and there was no sign of people that they were alone. Assuming could get them all killed.

They were halfway back to the vehicle when they heard the revving of a truck's engine. They came around the corner of the hotel at a dead run. Harper had picked Olivia up in her arms and was sprinting back toward the jeep.

Liam was bolting across the parking area as Harper reached the back seat of the car and plopped Olivia inside.

"Six men," Liam said. "Probably all armed. At least two are headed this way."

"What do you suggest we do?"

"They know this area, and we don't. I suggest we go. Now."

Jack had climbed into the back seat of the jeep, next to his sister. His eyes were as big as saucers. The fear was back, and who could blame him? Cade was scared too.

Harper met his eyes and nodded once.

They were good.

They'd get out of this.

They had the jeep, an ex-military guy with a rifle, and Harper with both her handguns. They also had two precious souls in the back seat. There was no way that Cade would allow anyone to hurt those children.

And he remembered in that moment something that he had learned in the barrio. He could kill to protect those he loved. He would kill if he had to.

But given another choice, he'd take it. There was no shame in running. In fact, wisdom dictated that they run.

"Get in," he shouted.

He started the engine, relieved by its roar.

There was nothing for them in Van Horn. They could only hope Alpine would be better.

Chapter 17

H ARPER'S PULSE ACCELERATED AS adrenaline spiked through her veins. She checked Olivia, whose eyes were wide and frightened as she clutched her dolls and stuck her thumb in her mouth.

Had they walked into a trap?

How?

How would anyone know they were coming this direction? Or was Van Horn simply a net, a convenient crossroads, an easy location to catch those driving through Texas as they searched desperately for a safe place?

Jack spoke to his sister in a low voice, trying to comfort her.

Harper met Cade's eyes as he glanced back at her. They were going to be okay. They would find a way out of this, as they'd found their way out of a dozen similar situations before.

They'd survived the barrio.

They'd survived the journey east.

They'd survived the hike to Guadalupe Peak and the soldiers who lay in wait and the race south. They would not be stopped by six assholes with an affinity for spray paint.

"We need to go." Cade's voice was filled with urgency and warning and a strength which rose up to meet Harper's fears.

Harper double-checked that Olivia's seatbelt was fastened. She heard the click of Jack's seatbelt, then glanced up to see that Liam had taken up a shooting position near the back driver's side door.

Cade revved the jeep's engine, and Harper breathed a silent prayer of thanksgiving for the vehicle. She ducked back down to do a final check of the children, to make sure they were safely buckled. Later she would wonder why she had done that. Some twenty-first century programming in her brain? Some part of her psyche that insisted a car wreck might be the most dangerous thing they'd face?

She was standing up straight, her hand on the door about to shut it, when three men appeared at the end of the alley. Liam took out the two on his side. Harper pulled her weapon, sighted in the person directly in front of her and fired at the same time that he did.

He dropped to the ground.

And Harper was thrown back by the force of the bullet impacting her arm. Liam was at her side instantly, pushing her into the front seat, slamming the door, racing around to the back. Cade peeled out as the vehicle they'd been hearing screeched to a stop in front of them.

Cade slammed the jeep into reverse and again punched the accelerator. Harper heard and felt the thump-thump of the tires running over one of the men they had shot. The jeep's tires squealed as they catapulted out onto the road. Cade threw the jeep into drive, and they lurched forward into the night.

Olivia was crying.

Jack was telling her everything would be okay.

Harper felt giddy and nauseous and confused all at the same time. Adrenaline continued to flood her bloodstream. She could feel her heart beat fast and strong. She could practically hear it. They'd done it. They'd operated as a team and escaped. She wanted to shout and punch the air. She wanted to tell Cade to stop so she could take the children in her arms.

She turned to see Liam hanging out his window, carefully aiming at the truck that was gaining on them. With two shots, he took out the front tires. The driver lost control as the truck slid and spun and finally smashed into an abandoned car.

"She's hit." Liam ejected the magazine from his pistol and slammed in a fresh one. "Cade, Harper is hit. Right arm."

He again positioned himself half out of the window.

"You're hit?" Cade's gaze shifted from her to the road to her again.

She saw the speedometer hit a hundred miles per hour. She reminded herself that she'd buckled both Olivia and Jack into their seats. They'd be okay. Even if they crashed, they'd be okay.

They wouldn't crash though.

They couldn't crash.

Cade was driving. They would not crash.

"We have one more asshole pretty far back."

"Harper, are you hit?"

Harper's left hand went to her right arm, upper bicep. She pulled away her hand and stared down at her fingers. Through the moon's light slanting through the jeep's sunroof she saw her hand, her fingers, but she couldn't comprehend what it meant. She rubbed her fingertips together.

They were wet with her blood.

They were stained red with her blood.

She was hit?

Cade fumbled in the bag at his feet, pulled out a t-shirt, and pushed it into her hands. "Put pressure on the wound, Harper."

She saw him glance in the rearview, saw the look of panic and indecision on his face.

"We need to stop."

"Now?"

"I need to get her in the back seat lying down or she could bleed out."

"Do it."

To Harper it felt like the time she'd been on a bumpy flight into San Diego International Airport. They'd slammed down on the rainy runway, and she'd been sure they were going to slide right off the tarmac. Slide into the night.

She pulled the t-shirt away and saw that it, too, was now wet and red. Her teeth began to chatter, and she felt suddenly cold.

Olivia was still crying. Why was Olivia crying?

Jack was talking to his sister, his voice low and steady and scared. Harper could hear that beneath everything else. He was such a good boy. Why hadn't she told him that?

"Unbuckle your sister, Jack. Get up front. Both of you. Hurry."

And then Cade dashed around the front of the jeep, threw open her door, and picked her up as if she weighed nothing. As if she were a breeze drifting across the Chihuahuan desert. She felt that whisper of air on her face and closed her eyes.

"Huh-uh. Eyes open, sweetheart." He slipped her into the back seat.

"Buckle the kids," she muttered, struggling to remain conscious.

"Done," Liam assured her. Liam was driving. Where were the kids?

"Stop crying, Olivia." Jack's voice was kind but authoritative.

He was such a good brother. Harper wanted to tell him that, but the words wouldn't come.

"Liam's going to get us out of here," Jack continued. "Harper's going to be okay."

And then, for a moment, everything went dark.

When she woke, Cade was crouched beside her—half on the seat, half in the floorboard. He was pushing the compress against her arm, talking to her. She couldn't make out what he was saying. She wanted to reach up though, reach up and wipe the worry from his face, tell him that they would be fine. He'd done it. He'd driven like Mario Andretti and they were free of...

The graffiti.

The men at the end of the alley.

Pulling her weapon and firing and watching the man fall.

The slap of the bullet into her arm.

She heard her voice, heard a groan that must be coming from her though it sounded nothing like her.

Cade put his face right up close to hers. "Breathe with me, baby. Breathe in and out. Your body needs the oxygen. Your heartrate needs to go down. Slow. With me."

And somehow she was able to do that. Somehow she was able to trust that if Cade said the most important thing right this moment was to focus on breathing in tandem with him, then it was. And she would.

Her arm now felt as if it was on fire.

When she tried to look at it, Cade's fingers turned her face back toward him. "With me, Harper. In...and out. That's it. That's good."

"I messed up."

"No, you didn't."

"I should have..." What should she have done? How could something so important slip from her mind? She should have...

Her eyes were impossibly heavy.

She wanted to stay awake. She wanted to do it for Cade.

But she needed to sleep, just for a moment.

She needed to rest.

Chapter 18

C ADE HADN'T QUESTIONED HIS ability to make a medical decision in many years. He was a competent doctor. He'd been trained well. He had plenty of experience. He had listened and learned and applied himself to the field of medicine. Now, he was holding the life of the woman he loved in his hands, and he wasn't sure he'd made the right decision.

He tried to remember how far it was to Alpine.

An hour? Two?

Harper was drifting in and out of consciousness. Olivia had fallen asleep. Jack kept turning in his seat and looking back at Cade, at Harper, then at Cade again. He wanted to assure the boy that she'd be fine, but he didn't want to lie to him. In truth, Cade had done everything he knew to stop the bleeding, but he feared it wasn't enough.

If they pulled over, the people pursuing them would most certainly catch up, and Harper might die. They all might die, depending on what the Watchmen wanted. If they continued hurtling down the road, Harper might bleed out.

"How close are we?"

"Twenty-six miles." Liam's voice was tight, controlled. He met Cade's gaze in the rearview mirror.

Cade shook his head.

Twenty-six miles.

Even at their current speed, it was too great a distance.

He didn't think Harper had that long. He looked out the jeep's window, saw that they were barreling through a deserted town. Marfa. They'd made it to Marfa, but no one was there. Some of the buildings were burned. All looked empty.

Liam never slowed. He pushed the jeep harder. The needle on the speedometer passed ninety, ninety-five, one hundred miles an hour. They flew through the abandoned town, in the middle of the desert, toward a destination that they had no reason to hope could or would save her.

Olivia woke and Cade was aware of Jack speaking to her in a low voice. He heard the little girl's cries, but his eyes, his attention remained on Harper.

Her eyes fluttered open. "The baby?"

"The baby will be fine." He nearly choked on the words. Harper had lost quite a bit of blood. His hands, her clothes, the seat of the jeep were covered with it.

He wasn't sure he could save her.

He wasn't sure he could save their child.

He needed to tie off the artery, remove the bullet, and give her a blood transfusion. He couldn't do any of those things in the back seat of a jeep, hurtling down a highway at one hundred miles per hour. He maintained pressure on the compress, waited for her eyes to focus on his again.

"The baby will be fine," he repeated. "Both of you will be fine, Harper."

It wasn't a lie, or so he told himself.

She needed to believe.

She needed to hold on.

Harper blinked. He wiped away her tears, and he tried to smile.

"Okay," she said, and then she closed her eyes.

Whether she believed him, or simply wanted to assuage his fears, he didn't know. Her heart rate was up. Her breathing was labored. Her skin was cool and pale. She wasn't disoriented, though—not yet. She was lucid when she was conscious. The human body was an amazing thing and could lose a full thirty percent of its blood before the heart would be unable to compensate. At forty percent, organ failure began, followed by coma and death.

Thirty percent could be corrected with a transfusion.

Harper's blood type was O+, the most common blood type in the United States. Unfortunately Cade was A+. He couldn't give his blood to her. Transfusing the wrong blood type would, in the end, do more harm than good.

He glanced out the window and saw nothing but high desert. In that moment, Cade was both exhausted and vibrating with desperate energy. He could save this woman. Give him an adequately stocked operating room, a sterile environment, a blood bank...

He had none of those things.

Harper again opened her eyes, attempted a weak smile, and squeezed his hand ever so lightly. It was like being touched by a butterfly. It was like feeling the brush of angel's wings. How would he possibly go on without her? What would be the point? And had they really survived the last three months, just to die on a rural highway in the middle of nowhere?

Then suddenly, as if she were sitting in the back seat with them, he heard Tía's voice.

You must protect her. You must protect the child that grows within her. You must see that they both reach a land where the child may thrive.

Had the old woman somehow known what they would face in the Guadalupe Mountains? How could the way north possibly have been worse? At least if they were trapped in the tent encampment, if they were abducted by their own military, they would be alive.

If you go north, you will not make it at all.

It's possibly the most important thing you'll ever do, but I have faith in you...

Tears slipped down his cheeks. When he raised a hand to brush them away, he realized Harper was staring at him. She didn't speak. She didn't tell him everything would be all right or ask him why he was crying. She simply looked at him, and that look—her eyes—held all the dreams that he'd held on to for their future even in this bleak world where they found themselves.

"There's a roadblock and armed guards," Liam said. "What do you want me to do?"

If they barreled through it, they'd be shot.

If they stopped, it would use up precious moments.

But what choice did they have?

"Anyone behind us?"

"They're pretty far back."

"Stop ten feet shy of the barricade."

The jeep slammed to a stop, and a tall, lean man stepped forward. His skin was tanned the color of the desert, and he sported a significant scar over his right eye.

He took one look into the front and back seats of the jeep. His gaze traveled past Liam, to the children, to Cade pressing the compress to Harper's right arm.

"What's her status?"

"Bullet wound to the right brachial," Cade said, surprised that his voice came out strong, efficient, professional—all things that he did not feel at this moment. "She's lost a lot of blood."

The man nodded once then turned to a kid who looked about twenty and sat atop a chestnut mare. "Dylan, take them to Doc Turner, fast as you can."

The kid turned his horse and bolted forward at a gallop.

The man with the scar slapped the top of the jeep, and Liam took off like a bullet from a gun. They burst through the barricade which had been opened for them, down the main thoroughfare and into the heart of Alpine.

Dylan stopped the horse so suddenly, Cade was surprised he didn't catapult over the reins like some character from a cartoon. They'd pulled up in front of an old train station. Dylan had been talking into a walkie talkie of some sort, and three people burst out of the main entry of the train station, guiding a stretcher.

A man who looked to be in his forties opened the back door of the jeep and squatted next to Harper. "My name is Doctor Turner. Can you tell me her status?"

"GSW to the brachial artery. Heart rate 120 and climbing. I think she's lost about..." and now his voice did betray him, cracked with the pain and the desperation of the thing. "She's lost close to thirty percent."

"Blood type?" The brown eyes searched his, seemed to convey that he understood and they'd find a way to save her.

"O positive." Cade swallowed. "I'm A positive."

The doctor turned to the young man wearing a Sul Ross t-shirt. "Get Tanda."

Then he turned to the girl, who couldn't have been over twenty. "We'll work the sheet under her and move her to the stretcher on three."

Cade backed out of the jeep, nearly falling when he stood as the free flow of blood sent the feeling of pins and needles to his feet.

"You okay?" Liam was at his elbow, supporting him.

"Fine. Just—my legs fell asleep."

Jack and Olivia remained huddled in the front passenger seat, the safety belt still buckled around them.

"It's going to be okay," Cade said.

Jack nodded, and Olivia clutched her dolls more tightly. Then Cade's attention was pulled back to Harper.

"One, two, three." They moved Harper smoothly onto the stretcher, then hustled her into the train station.

Cade turned to Liam. "You'll watch the kids?"

"Of course."

Cade needed to be inside, needed to be next to Harper, but he had to do something else first. "Thank you, Liam. I'm sorry about the..." He nodded to his jaw.

Liam grinned. "Not a problem. I deserved it. Now go."

He jogged toward the entry of the train station, which had very clearly been converted to an emergency triage center. There were so many thoughts running through his mind at once, that he felt dizzy with them.

If they'd left Guadalupe National Park without Liam, Harper would have died.

If they'd gone north as they'd originally planned, the children would have died. They wouldn't, couldn't, have survived on the mountain alone.

Alpine had a doctor and a triage center.

Harper had a chance.

He hurried into the building, passing a dog that was part Labrador and seemed to be guarding the place. Cade had to blink twice when he pushed past the curtain to the enclosed area where they'd taken her.

"Wash up and Akule will get you a gown." Turner was snapping on gloves and already had a surgical mask covering his face.

By the time Cade had washed up and donned the gown, someone had started an IV in Harper's left arm. Her right arm was laid out across an instrument tray and had already been draped. "I could use some help," Turner said.

Both Akule and Cade jumped.

"Akule, monitor her vitals..." His eyes rose to Cade's, assessing him and deciding quickly. "Can you assist?"

"Yes."

They clamped off the artery, found and removed the bullet, cleaned the area, sutured the artery back together, and closed the incision with eight neat stitches. Mercifully, Harper slept through it all. They must have given her something. Her breathing was smooth, even, and when Cade glanced at Akule she confirmed what he hoped. "Heart rate is down to ninety."

At that moment a young woman ducked in past the curtain. She was calm, self-assured, and beautiful. Without any directions, she sat in a chair next to Harper and began squeezing and releasing her fist. Akule tore open a field blood transfusion kit, tied a band around her arm, cleaned her skin with disinfectant, and slipped a needle into her antecubital vein.

"O positive?" Cade asked.

Her eyes remained calm, compassionate, understanding. "O negative, actually."

"That will work." His legs nearly gave out then. He stumbled backwards and collapsed into a chair that the boy pushed toward him at the last minute.

"My name is Tanda Lopez, and I'm the police chief of Alpine."

Her blood—rich, red, and perfectly suited for Harper—ran through the tube, into a blood bag from the emergency triage kit, then up and into the IV that had been placed in Harper's arm.

"You've done this before." Cade couldn't quite grasp what he was seeing here. He couldn't believe that this was real, that it wasn't a fantasy he'd conjured with his mind. He feared he would wake and find himself sitting by Harper's lifeless body on the side of the road.

The woman's voice brought him back. "Doc Turner has an efficient triage center set up here, and unfortunately, we've had a bit of experience."

She didn't say anything else, but her eyes told him that she understood. That in this dark world, this time of complete anarchy and confusion, there were still havens to be found. There were still people willing and able to help. And to Cade, that meant there was hope, not just for Harper or him or the two children waiting with Liam.

Hope for everyone.

And that kind of hope?

That provided a light powerful enough to send a beacon across the desert, through the mountains, and beyond.

Chapter 19

H ARPER WOKE THREE DIFFERENT times before she became fully conscious. The first two times she saw Cade sitting beside her bed, head back, sound asleep. The third time she saw Liam, who smiled at her and said, "Hey." All three times her eyes were incredibly heavy, and though she wanted to speak, wanted to stay awake and ask a dozen questions, she couldn't.

Sleep, sweet sleep, pulled her back under.

The fourth time she woke, Jack was sitting by her bed, looking anxious, watching her as if she might vanish before his eyes. She smiled, or tried to, and his eyes lit up.

She blinked herself fully awake. "How ya doing, Jack?" The words felt gravely coming from her throat.

"I'm okay. Are you okay?"

"Yeah." She tried to put conviction in her voice. "Where's Cade? Liam?"

"They finally went to get something to eat. They've been taking turns in here since yesterday. I guess you were better, so they said I could stay. I'm supposed..." His eyes darted toward the door. "Supposed to go and tell someone if you wake up."

"In a minute." Her mind was clearing as they spoke. She needed a few minutes to get her bearings, and she wanted to erase the fear in his eyes.

"We're in Alpine?"

"Yeah. This was the train station, but I guess now it's like a hospital or something."

"I remember a man with..." She tried to move her right arm, found it was bandaged and incredibly heavy—too heavy. Instead, she raised her left and touched a point above her right eye.

"A scar? That was the vet. His name is Logan. I guess he's been helping the doctor. Doc Turner runs this place, and he has a dog named Zeus." Jack's words sputtered to a stop.

"I was scared," he admitted, brushing at his eyes with the back of his hand. "I was scared you might die, like Mom did."

"I think I'm going to be okay."

"That's what Cade said. I wanted to believe him, but..."

"Cade won't lie to you. Ever." Harper tried to swallow and found her throat was painfully dry. She nodded toward the glass with a straw in it.

Jack jumped up, helped her with it, and when she'd finished, he smiled at her as if she'd done something amazing. "That's good. They said you needed to drink."

She noticed a band-aid across the back of her hand. "Superhero band-aid. Cool."

"We found that, in the other town, before the shooting started. Even after we got here, Olivia wouldn't stop crying. She wouldn't believe you were okay. So, we gave her the band-aid and she put it on your hand, and it...it made her feel better. That's stupid, I guess."

"It's not stupid."

"Cade told me the two rules of scavenging."

"Yeah?"

"Take what you find..."

"When you find it." She smiled and nodded.

"And never assume you're alone. I guess that's what we did wrong in that other town." His lower lip started to tremble and he bit down on it.

"Hey, Jack. Look at me, hon." He finally did, and she said, "Even if we'd driven straight through that town, the same thing could have happened. Or worse. Instead, we're all here, and we're all okay."

"Right."

"Right."

"I should...I should go and get Cade."

"Okay."

He was nearly to the far side of the room, when she called him back. "How do you like it here?"

"I like it. If we stay, Olivia can go to school here. We both can."

"Then I think we should stay."

Jack's concerned expression finally turned to a smile, and he looked like the ten-year-old boy he was. "Cool."

Harper placed a hand against her stomach, hoping to feel a flutter though she knew it was too early for that. Was her baby okay? Surely if he, or she, wasn't, she would know. She'd be able to tell. She'd feel the loss of it.

She stared up at the ceiling and tried to piece together the last twenty-four hours—driving into Van Horn, the ambush, a searing pain in her arm... She turned her head and studied her arm, but all she could see was a bandage. Her memories after she was shot were blurry. Cade picking her up and placing her in the back seat of the jeep, the kids crying, Liam's face somber and concerned.

Cade bending over her in the back seat.

Cade promising her the baby would be fine.

She again touched her stomach, laid her hand there. And though she didn't feel a flutter or a kick, she said, "Hello, little one."

When Cade burst into the room she knew, in one look at him, she knew that their child was fine. He wouldn't be smiling at her that way unless the baby was okay. His hair was a mess, and his eyes more tired than she'd ever seen before. He looked to her as if he'd lost another few pounds. She supposed they all had.

"Hey." He pulled the chair closer to her bed, picked up her left hand, and kissed it. "How are you feeling?"

"Thirsty."

He laughed and held the cup for her to sip from. "You gave us quite a scare."

"What happened? I only remember...flashes."

"We were ambushed by a group called the Watchmen. They chased us all the way from Van Horn, but they fell away as we closed in on Alpine's roadblock."

"And we're in a train station?" She glanced around her room. Medical charts were pinned to the walls. Sheets had been hung on rods to give the illusion of privacy.

"They've turned it into a triage center. What they've done here in Alpine.. .it's pretty amazing." Something caught in Cade's throat—fear or gratitude or disbelief. "You lost a lot of blood. I didn't know how...I couldn't imagine..." He stared down at the floor.

Harper squeezed his hand and waited.

"As I knelt beside you in that back seat, I prayed for an operating room and a blood bank." His laugh was a short bark. "Foxhole prayer. That's what it was. First one I've uttered in a long time."

His eyes met hers, and Harper wondered at how deeply she loved this man that she'd known for such a short time.

"They've blood-typed every person in the town. They even have a card catalog that contains every person's basic information. Remember those old card catalogs like you'd see in the library? If you needed a book, you'd walk over to the drawer, find the correct letter, pull it out, and thumb through the cards."

Harper nodded. Most libraries had gone digital by the time she started searching for particular books, but she remembered the long wooden cabinets with the little drawers, letters of the alphabet neatly typed and slipped into the label holder. Her elementary school had been slow to modernize.

"By the time Miles removed the bullet in your arm, Tanda was here to give you a blood transfusion." He ran both hands over his face, then scooted closer, the smile on his face genuine now. "They saved you, Harper. You and the baby."

"You saved me."

He shook his head. "I kept you alive, but I couldn't save you. I couldn't give you my blood. It's just one more example of why we can't survive in this world alone. We need each other, and Alpine...I think it might be the place we were looking for."

"Jack said they have school here."

"They do."

"Then we'll stay."

"Okay. We'll stay."

Harper didn't want to sleep. She wanted to look at Cade. She wanted to see Olivia and Liam and this woman named Tanda and the doctor who had saved her. She wanted to ask more questions, but she was suddenly terribly exhausted. She fell into a deep sleep with Cade still holding her hand and the hope that he was describing taking root in her heart.

Chapter 20

T HREE DAYS AFTER THEY arrived, Liam, Cade, and Harper met with
Alpine's Council. The day had turned unexpectedly cold, and rain
splashed on the pavement outside the window. The Academic Building of the
Sul Ross University sat on a hill on the north side of town. The windows
afforded a view of the circular drive, the parking area, and the town beyond.
Liam studied and assessed the people around him.

The council, which had been voted on by the entire community, consisted
of a few people they knew and a few people they didn't. Tanda Lopez—chief
of police, Miles Turner—the doctor who had saved Harper, and Logan
Wright—the veterinarian who had met them at the barrier.

Logan had made the on-the-spot decision to let them in. He hadn't hesitated,
and that had been as instrumental to saving Harper's life as the doctor's skill.

Liam could tell these three had been the core group which helped Alpine
adjust to the post-modern world...a term that his military unit had used to
describe the world they were currently living in.

As for the situation in Alpine, Tanda, Miles, and Logan had apparently acted
when the mayor wouldn't. They'd been decisive, and they'd put the needs of
Alpine first. They were solid.

Ron Mullins, Dixie Peters, and Emmanuel Garcia had been city employees
who had aligned on the right side of things. Keme Lopez was Tanda's brother.
Liam wasn't sure that meant he was trustworthy. The man's expression was hard
and inscrutable.

Gonzo Watson was added to the council after Keme's wife had died when
Alpine was attacked two months earlier. In a previous life, Liam would have

dismissed Gonzo as an old hippy, but something in the old guy's eyes told Liam that he'd do well not to dismiss this man too early.

Then there was Jackson Castillo—an old rancher who owned a large spread outside of town. Liam would have to speak with Jackson in private. Jackson would have to be dealt with, one way or another.

"The council meets with newcomers. We've found it's best to explain our expectations of each family, each person, up front. Should you have a problem with those expectations, you're free to continue on." Tanda waited until Cade, Harper, and Liam had nodded that they understood. "Also, as you can imagine, we don't receive much information as to what's happening in the world."

"We provide information. You provide safe harbor." Cade's tone was non-judgmental, simply stating it as he saw it.

Tanda shrugged, but she didn't contradict him. Instead, she nodded to Dixie Peters.

Peters looked to be in her late twenties or early thirties and wore her blonde hair pulled back in a hairband.

"I'm the fire chief in Alpine. It's a challenge to fight fires when we have no running water, but we're doing okay. Should you decide to stay, you'll be required to sit through a one-hour fire prevention class taught by one of my personnel and another hour-long class on how we fight fires with sand, blankets, basically anything we have. These two requirements are just that—required."

She glanced out the window at the falling rain, then smiled. "Obviously it isn't a problem right now, but we do have our dry spells and fire...it's as big a threat to our existence as attacks from surrounding communities."

They'd obviously done this type of *Welcome to Alpine* session several times. Emmanuel Garcia, the county health director, took up where Dixie left off, explaining that they had limited food and medical reserves and that they'd scoured area facilities to inventory and collect anything of use. "Those who have chosen to remain in the area are committed to making those reserves last and adding to them whenever possible."

Ron Mullins spoke next. He looked to be past retirement age. Before June 6th, he'd been Alpine's public works director. "Every family is required to collect water when it's raining, and ration it when things are dry. Every family is expected to plant a vegetable garden..."

"A victory garden," Harper whispered.

"Something like that, yes. We were fortunate in that we had a good supply of heirloom seeds that we were able to disburse throughout the community. Since we have no supplies coming into Alpine, it's critical to our survival that we grow what we need."

Tanda studied her group, pride evident in the way she looked at each one, then she cleared her throat and picked up the narrative. "Keme acts as a liaison between the Hispanic, Kiowa, and white communities."

"I also teach classes on the old ways." His grin was a bit wolfish and didn't quite extend to his eyes.

"Such as?" Liam asked.

"Archery, natural medicines, edible plants, even meditation..."

"The meditation has been critical," Miles admitted. "Given that we have no anti-depressants, no alcohol or drugs, it was important that we address mental health issues early."

"Jackson coordinates with outlying ranchers who are able to provide hay for the horses and water from the springs when we needed it last summer." Tanda glanced at Gonzo and smiled. "As for Gonzo, he managed to bridge an agreement between the artist community and the rest of Alpine."

Gonzo ran his fingers through his white beard, but he didn't speak. There was a story there, Liam was sure—one that he hoped to hear eventually.

"That covers the main points of life in Alpine. Tell us about El Paso."

Liam and Harper looked to Cade.

He sat up straighter, craned his neck to the left and the right, then met Tanda's gaze head on.

"The northern barrio was a result of desperation and need. The hospital I worked at closed in days after the event. There wasn't enough personnel to keep it open. When all technology went down, things went apocalyptic pretty fast...looting, carjacking, larceny, even killing." He glanced at Harper when he said the last part.

"I was outside the barrio for the first few weeks," Harper added. "Cade isn't overstating how bad things were. Nearly seven hundred thousand people lived in the El Paso region prior to June 6th. Plus there's an international border crossing. When I realized what happened wasn't temporary, I made my way to the barrio. I'd heard that they were allowing people in, and they did."

"What did you do before?" Logan asked.

She smiled, and Liam saw the sadness in it. The realization that the world she had built was forever gone. "I was a writer—romance, primarily."

No one spoke. No one laughed, but no one spoke.

Tanda sat forward, pressed her hands together, and looked directly at Harper. "We need teachers here, and we also need someone to document what is happening. Peggy Looper at the university is spearheading a project to record in detail every aspect of this world we find ourselves in. I'd like you to help her. It might not be as fun as what you wrote before, but it's critical to the current and the next generation."

Harper nodded, rubbing a hand against her stomach.

Tanda turned to Cade. "Why did you leave the barrio?"

"Supplies were diminishing, the number of refugees continued to grow, and then we learned of Harper's pregnancy. We'd heard of a new community in Cloudcroft."

"New Mexico?" Jackson shook his head. "You headed the wrong direction."

"Yeah, that's another story. Suffice to say, we ended up going east where we became aware of an entirely different threat." He shook his head.

Liam realized that Cade was still struggling with what they'd all seen at the top of Guadalupe Peak. He was as well.

"That other threat..." Cade shook his head. "I think Liam can explain that better than I can."

Everyone turned their attention to Liam, and he realized it was now or never. Yes, they might throw him out, but if that was the worst they did, he'd be fine.

He didn't want to be on the outside of this though.

He wanted to be in the middle of it.

He wanted to stay in Alpine.

Chapter 21

C ADE WATCHED LIAM AS he sat forward and let his gaze fall on each person in the group. Finally, he nodded as if to himself, and started to tell his story, a story that Cade was very interested in hearing.

"I was stationed at Fort Bliss on June 6th."

"Rank?" Logan asked.

"E-8. Master Sergeant."

Logan nodded and indicated for him to continue.

"We understood almost immediately that the satellites were down." He paused. "You know about that?"

Tanda nodded. "We visited McDonald Observatory. They told us about the Kessler Event. Basically, they described it as uncontrolled collisions that cascaded into a complete collapse."

Cade raised his hand. "Hang on. This is the first I'm hearing about satellites."

"According to the scientists at the observatory, the sheer number of satellites and space junk orbiting the Earth created an unsustainable environment."

"Unsustainable how?"

"Dr. Scott, the director of the observatory, compared it to a crowded freeway."

"Only the objects above us were travelling at speeds in excess of 28,000 kilometers per hour." Liam shrugged as if to say, *What can you do?*

"Right," Tanda sat back, crossing her arms and stared out the window, as if she could see into the past. As if she could peer into a world they no longer inhabited. "Once the first collision happened, the other satellites fell like a set of dominoes. It had even been predicted, by this scientist named Dr. Kessler."

"That's why the infrastructure went down?" Harper pressed her fingertips to her lips.

"According to Dr. Scott, satellites control GPS, so that explains plane crashes. Some were able to land safely, but many couldn't. It affected everything from streetlights to trains. Those things were—essentially—caused by GPS failure."

Logan Wright continued the explanation. "Communications, power grids, financial district, even things as simple as glucose monitors that send your blood sugar level to your Apple watch. From a personal level all the way to a global one, things cascaded to a stop."

No one spoke for a moment.

Sometimes the sheer enormity of how life had changed was hard to grasp.

Cade thought Liam understood that. He waited, before describing his own personal hell on June 6th.

"Good description, I guess." Liam sat up straighter. "Anyway, everything was down, and we were aware of that within the first hour. The US Army has upper-level satellites. Some were working and some weren't. Don't ask me why. It's not my area of expertise."

"What is your area?" Keme asked.

"Acquisition of personnel in times of civil collapse."

"That's a specialty?" Harper shook her head. "Wow."

"We held mock exercises, even kept dossiers on key civilians in the area. My area was El Paso, and I quickly realized the northern barrio was the place to find most of the people I needed."

Tanda was watching him intensely. "What did you do when you found them?"

"If I thought they'd be amenable to transferring into the military compound, I approached them directly."

"And if they weren't...amenable?" Mile's expression was grim, as if he couldn't quite believe what he was hearing.

"We used whatever means necessary to persuade those unwilling to come with us."

Cade felt suddenly nauseous.

He'd known whatever Liam had to confess was going to be bad, but he hadn't quite envisioned this. Since Liam had shown him the tracking device as they stood outside the children's tent, Cade had known that Liam's secrets would be terrible, tragic even. Cade's mind had gone back over the people who'd left the barrio in the middle of the night, people he would never have predicted would strike out on their own. Turned out, they hadn't. They'd been moved out of the barrio by Liam.

"You have to understand, this wasn't just about you and me, or El Paso, or even the US Army." Liam's voice had taken on a harder edge. "This was a worldwide event, and players on the global stage took full advantage of it."

"Meaning what?" Tanda asked.

"Meaning that within six hours of the collapse, we were attacked by domestic and foreign entities."

Everyone started talking at once then.

Tanda finally raised her hand to quiet them. "Go on."

"I can't give you specifics. I don't even know specifics. However, the scenario we'd been planning for, preparing for, had happened. My job was to help plug the holes."

"Plug the holes?" Cade's temper spiked. He seriously considered taking another swing at Liam.

"We needed doctors, Cade. Hell, we even needed writers. The last estimates I saw were that the U.S. alone experienced a twenty-four percent fatality rate on June 6th."

"How?" Tanda asked, her voice quiet, low, waiting. "Tell us how that was possible."

Liam began ticking the possibilities off his fingers. "Comms were out almost immediately, as well as traffic signals, 9-1-1, all public transportation. Train crashes, plane crashes—you know something about that here. I saw the wreckage outside of town. Urban areas also had to deal with folks stuck in elevators or trapped in cars from multi-vehicle collisions. Basically your worst nightmare."

"And we thought we had it bad here in Alpine." Dixie Peters sat forward, elbows on her knees, fingertips massaging her temples. "I haven't really allowed myself to imagine what it must have been like in El Paso or Dallas or Houston."

"Or New York City." Liam rolled his shoulders, stretched his neck to the left, then the right.

Cade was certain that these were facts the man didn't relish sharing. Somehow sharing the chaos of those days caused him to relive the tragedies he'd seen, experienced, and been unable to stop.

"The more unsavory element seized the opportunity to plunder anything nearby. Metropolitan areas across the country very quickly faced uncontrolled fires. Medical institutions—like Cade's hospital—were soon overwhelmed. Within a week, communities were facing a lack of emergency personnel and medical supplies, scarcity of water and food, marked increase in crime...."

Keme was the one who finally spoke, finally broke the stunned silence. "As the satellites fell into an uncontrolled cascade of destruction, so did our societal structures."

"Exactly." Liam ran a hand over his face. "And that's why I was on board with what I was ordered to do. I understood my mission, and I was willing to complete it."

"That all changed when we went east to Guadalupe." Cade explained about the town they'd passed through, about Cochiece's story, the journal, the tent city, Jack and Olivia and their mother Ashley.

"So you were kidnapping Cade and Harper?" Miles looked incredulous. "How is it that you're still with them? And what makes you think that we'd want to allow you to stay in Alpine?"

Which started another round of side conversations that Tanda finally raised her hand to stop. "Let him finish."

"Cade's right. When I heard Cochiece's story, I began to suspect I'd been misled. The journal...well I wasn't willing to be swayed by what sounded like a teenaged girl's writing, but it bothered me. It was one more piece of the puzzle." He stopped, cleared his throat, stared at the floor, and finally pushed on. "Then

I saw the tent city in the desert. They had women, children, men…and they were being guarded. That wasn't what I signed up for."

"So you're AWOL now? You've been doing the Army's bidding since June 6th, but now you've turned your back on your orders?" Ron Mullins shook his head in disbelief. "We're supposed to take your word on that?"

Liam continued staring at the floor. Finally, he looked up and met Tanda's gaze. "The tent city changed everything in my mind. Then we found the kids. We learned that some military guy had shot Ashley in the back. I was there when she died. The military that I work for, that I'm a member of, would never have done such a thing. That woman posed no threat to anyone. Shooting her makes no sense."

No one spoke.

Finally Tanda asked, "So you're saying that someone else is in charge now? Someone you don't trust?"

"Maybe. I don't know how high up it goes. I didn't exactly have time to stay around and ask questions. They were actively hunting Cade and Harper by that point. We had to get out of there."

Cade picked up the story, told how Liam had taken the tracker, hiked an alternate trail, and sent the people pursuing them off in the wrong direction.

There was complete silence for a moment, then two.

Finally Tanda sighed. "I'm not in charge of Alpine, though I take personal responsibility for the safety of the people here. Still, it's not up to me who stays and who goes. The council votes, and only a unanimous vote results in an invitation to stay."

"And I'll respect that decision." Liam let his gaze scan the entire group. "If the problem is me…my past…then you should at least consider letting the others stay, and I'll continue on. I think I could be an asset here, but I can't be if you don't trust me."

Tanda nodded, then looked at her group.

Cade found himself wondering what he would do if they said no. Where would he take Harper? How would he keep her safe as they made their way back past the Watchmen and then the US military? How would they ever make it to Cloudcroft?

"Does anyone have any follow-up questions?"

They had been sitting in a sort of oblong circle. No one had any questions.

"Okay. When you vote, please stipulate whether it's for the whole group or the group minus Liam." Tanda started with the person to Harper's right, the other doctor in the group—Miles Turner.

"I vote in favor of allowing them all to stay."

One by one, they went around the circle, and only two hesitated—Tanda's brother Keme and the old rancher named Jackson. Both pierced Liam with a look, pulled in a deep breath, then raised their right hand and voted for the entire group to be included.

Tanda stood, walked over to Liam, and shook his hand. "I believe you're on the right side of things now, and we need someone who's been on the inside. We need to understand what's happening. We could use you here in Alpine."

Her gaze drifted over Harper, then Cade. "We could use all of you. If you want to stay, you're welcome."

They shook hands all around, and Cade thought it was over then. Instead, Tanda took her seat again. She sat erect, her dark eyes betraying nothing. Cade understood that this was Tanda the chief of police, not Tanda the welcome committee.

"Now tell us about the Watchmen."

Temporary housing had been set up in the high school gym. There were cots, a kitchen stocked with supplies that they were welcome to use, and bathrooms with toilets that still flushed, though water had to be carried in one pail at a time, then transferred into the toilet's tank.

For Cade, walking into the gymnasium was almost painful. The smell of sweaty athletes and dirty gym socks and popcorn persisted under whatever had been used to clean the place. Cade was instantly taken back to his high school days, pep rallies, and Friday night lights.

It was a world he'd worked very hard to forget.

They did their best to wash off the dust and grime of the road. Jack and Olivia were asleep within minutes of lying down. Cade, Harper, and Liam moved three of the plastic chairs into a tight circle a few feet away—close enough to hear the kids if needed, far enough that their discussion wouldn't wake them.

The first topic they broached was the Watchmen.

Liam sat back, arms crossed, legs stretched out in front of him. "I'm surprised they had as much information about the Watchmen as they did."

"This town has a university," Harper pointed out. "It sounds to me like the council is putting it to good use."

Cade stretched and laced his hands behind his head. "The campus provides more than meeting rooms and dorms. It also houses a whole lot of information."

"I can't believe this Peggy Harper was able to find a set of discs that contained encyclopedias." Harper shook her head. "Old school."

Liam laughed. "Very old school. How did they find anything that would read a disc?"

"That's the thing about when a town pulls together." Cade had been thinking about this. He'd been considering the advantages and disadvantages of staying with a larger group like the one in Alpine. "You know there was some octogenarian out there who had an old computer in the closet with a disc drive. Then it was just a matter of a computer whiz-kid figuring out how to make it run."

Liam's expression turned serious. "How did a comic book writer inspire an anarchist cult?"

"Alan Moore isn't just any comic book writer," Harper pointed out. "*V for Vendetta*, *Swamp Thing*, and of course *Watchmen*…they were big. He became famous precisely because his works depicted a dystopian, post-apocalyptic future."

"Yeah, but when these guys—the assholes who ravaged Van Horn—began following him, the apocalypse hadn't happened yet." Liam shook his head. "I don't get it. How does someone become a cult leader in a post-modern world?"

"I suspect our Van Horn criminals were into Watchmen well before the satellites fell. What was it Tanda said? Something about Moore's opinion on conspiracy theories..." Cade knew he was tired and needed sleep. He snapped his fingers and still it didn't come to him.

Harper smiled and pulled her long, auburn hair behind her shoulders. It was the first time he'd seen it down since they'd left the barrio.

"According to Tanda, who was quoting this Peggy Looper—the head of the Sul Ross library—Moore believed that people bought into conspiracy theories because it was more comforting than the alternative."

"That's it." Cade sat up straighter. "That the truth is more frightening, and the truth is—"

"No one is in control," Liam finished for him. "Our man Alan Moore was a true-blue nihilist."

Harper rubbed the small of her back and yawned. "It's easy to forget how quickly a conspiracy theory or a subversive group would gain credence before June 6th. Thanks largely to social media and the internet's biggest search engines, the echo chamber was still alive and well."

"It sounds as if the council plans to go on the offense as far as the Watchmen go."

"I'd love to be here to see it," Liam admitted. "I'd love to be a part of that."

Cade stared at the ceiling a minute, glanced at the kids, then sat forward with his elbows on his knees. "The council voted us in, but that doesn't mean we have to stay. Staying or leaving, that needs to be a decision that we actively make independent of any council, independent of anyone but ourselves. So let's discuss that. What are your feelings about staying? Harper?"

He noticed that whenever Harper was seriously considering a topic, she placed her hand on her stomach. He'd seen it a thousand times before with pregnant women, but seeing it with Harper...that was different. It touched him to the core, every single time.

"My first inclination is to say of course we'll stay. There's at least a semblance of law and order here, and the kids—the kids could go to school."

Cade waited. He let her dig for what was bothering her.

"We should see for ourselves, though. We should spend tomorrow finding out as much as we can about Alpine."

"Agreed." Cade turned to Liam. "Your decision is independent of ours. We've been through a lot together, but you need to do what's best for you."

Liam seemed to consider that a minute. "For better or worse, I've started thinking of us as the three musketeers. I understand what you're saying, Cade. There may come a time when our paths separate, but I don't think that time is now. And I agree with Harper. Hearing about a place is one thing, seeing it for ourselves might be something else completely."

"It's decided then." Cade glanced around the gym. There were only two other groups there that night.

Would they stay or move on?

How did someone make such a decision in this world they found themselves in? Nothing was certain, and he wasn't sure if anything was what it appeared to be.

"We stay or go together," he finally said. "And we make the decision after we thoroughly check out Alpine."

Chapter 22

L IAM WASN'T SURE EXACTLY where he was going to start his part of Discover Alpine, but fortunately someone showed up looking for him early the next morning. Liam was a little surprised that it was Stan Makowski, one of Tanda's officers, and he was carrying an infant baby girl.

"I'm on Chloe patrol." Stan jostled the baby girl on his shoulder. "My wife teaches at the school in the mornings, and my duty shift begins at 3:00. I have the pleasure of Chloe's company until lunch."

Stan was there to give Liam a tour of their perimeter. "Heard you might be a new recruit for helping in that area."

"I might be," Liam said, shaking his hand.

Stan was under six feet and probably weighed one-sixty. He had the look of a man who had trimmed down recently. His buckle was cinched tight and his shirt several sizes too big.

He turned to Cade. "Doc Turner was hoping to see you in his office. It's a couple of doors down from the police office. Easy to find."

"Sounds good to me."

Stan then turned his full attention to Harper.

"I heard what you've been through." He nodded at her arm. "If you want to take it easy today, no one would blame you."

"Actually, I'd like to become familiar with the town, if that's okay."

"Absolutely. Have a look around. Ask anyone if you have questions." He smiled at Jack and Olivia. "I have three kids. Two of them look about your age."

"I'm ten." Jack nodded toward his sister. "Olivia is six."

Instead of speaking to Stan, Olivia stepped closer to Harper.

"We have a daycare center over at the elementary school. It's only a mile from here."

Olivia reached for Harper's hand.

Harper smiled down at the little girl. "Thanks, but Olivia is going to spend the day with me today."

"Understandable. What about you, young man?"

Jack seemed surprised that he was given a choice. "I'd like to go with Cade, if that's okay."

"Sure thing. Families tend to take a few days to get settled before starting school and work. If there's anything you all need, let me or the person on duty here know."

Liam had shouldered his pack. "I'm ready if you are."

"Sure am. Glad to see you have your walking shoes on."

"Yeah, I broke them in on the road from El Paso to Guadalupe."

Both men laughed at the joke as they walked out of the gym. Liam understood quickly the gravity of the council's approval. If you were okayed to stay, you were also cleared to have any and all questions answered. Liam had been in the military too long to believe he was seeing everything, but he was seeing a lot of the structure and organization of Alpine.

They started with the Strategic Command Center, which was on the Sul Ross Campus. "Sul Ross had a healthy rodeo club, so this seemed the best place to quarter our horses." The place encompassed a lighted, covered arena, as well as an outdoor arena and sixty-two covered stalls.

"So you patrol via horseback?"

"Some. Officially Alpine is a little under five square miles. Early on, we set up neighborhood watch groups. They not only look out for mischief-makers, but they coordinate supplies, water when it's necessary to dispense it, and they meet weekly with residents in their area."

"Smart."

"We want to know about problems before they fester, and the neighborhood groups have been critical in that regard."

Liam again met Ron Mullins, Dixie Peters, and Emmanuel Garcia. They were cordial and busy, but they took the time to welcome him. More importantly, none of the alarm bells in his head sounded. Liam easily recognized a unit that operated well together.

This one did.

"You show up here and get your duty roster for the week," Stan explained. "If you're patrolling in town, you walk it. If you're farther out, one of the Sul Ross guys will issue you a horse."

"Sweet set up."

"Logan Wright saw early on how important livestock would be. He spends his morning here with the veterinarian and rodeo students. Afternoons he helps Doc Turner."

"Wouldn't be the apocalypse if we didn't have a vet working on people."

"Exactly."

"Firearms?"

"This is rural west Texas so most everyone has their own firearm. Some have rifles. Others have handguns. The problem, of course, is ammunition. Well, it's not a problem now, but it's something we're aware could be a problem in the future."

Stan shifted baby Chloe to his other shoulder. The little girl's eyes were open, and she was staring at Liam. It gave him a strange feeling. How long had it been since he'd seen an infant? Somewhere along the way he'd stopped believing in them, stopped believing that the next generation existed.

But of course it did.

They toured the supply center, which had everything from mess kits to saddles. Liam was surprised to see one area completely filled with archery supplies. When he asked Stan about it, the man shrugged and said, "Comes in handy when we send out hunting parties."

"How does that work?"

"Twice a month Ron meets with neighborhood coordinators to see how people are getting on in regard to food. Based on those needs, he'll call for a hunting party. Anyone who wants to go, can go. The food is divided up."

"Mule deer?"

"Yes. Mule deer is number one on the game list. We also have javelina, turkey, quail, dove, pronghorn, aoudad, and feral hogs."

"Sounds like a virtual meat market."

Stan laughed. "There may come a time when we hunt the mountain lions and even bear, but we'd rather not at this point. There's not enough of them, and hunting an animal into extinction won't help anyone. We still have cattle, of course, but again...we're careful how many we butcher. What we have, it needs to last."

"Do you use the compound bows for defense?"

"We haven't yet, but we're training to, just in case."

Which told Liam more that he needed to know. They were thinking ahead, they were conserving, and people were pulling their own weight.

"Met a guy named Jackson last night."

"Jackson Castillo. He has twenty-two sections outside of town."

"Sections?"

"A section is six hundred and forty acres or one square mile."

"And he has twenty-two?" Liam did the math in his head. Jackson owned fourteen thousand and eighty acres.

"They call it the big country for a reason."

Chloe had been fussing and now she began to cry with real vigor. They were still in the arena, and Stan stopped under a roof overhang. He dropped his backpack on the ground, fumbled through it, and pulled out a bottle of milk that was wrapped in a wet towel. "We don't have ice, but this seems to keep the milk from spoiling. At least it does now. Isn't so easy in the summer."

He plugged the bottle into Chloe's mouth, and the baby instantly stopped crying.

They stood there in the shade, watching the comings and goings of those on duty. Every one of them nodded or said hello to Stan. Liam supposed when your town's population was winnowed down to its most basic number, everyone knew everyone.

"You asked about Jackson. There is a man who is a bit of a puzzle to me. Jackson was what you might call a survivalist. He could probably have stayed on his acreage and done just fine." Stan kissed his daughter on the top of her head as she continued to suck from the bottle. "He didn't, though. He came into town and asked how he could help. He's older. He's stubborn, and he doesn't abide disrespect."

Liam smiled. "Sounds like my commanding officer."

Stan grunted. "He reminds me of Tanda a lot of times. She's a good boss, don't get me wrong, and I count her a close friend, but you do not want to get on the wrong side of that woman. She has one and only one mission each and every day. To defend Alpine. To see it...to see all of these people...through whatever it is we're going through."

Something in Stan's tone took Liam by surprise. "The satellite outage."

"Kessler Effect. Yeah, we've all been briefed on the cascade, and I have no doubt that's what started this situation. But now...now it's turned into something else entirely."

"Meaning what?"

"Meaning it's like we've been thrown back into pre-revolutionary times with each area, each town, fending for itself. But we're doing that with the knowledge and some of the technology of the twenty-first century."

"I'm not exactly sure what you're getting at."

Stan pulled the empty bottle from Chloe's mouth, tucked it into his backpack, shouldered the baby and rubbed her back in soft circles until a loud burp ensued.

Both men smiled.

"I guess what I mean is that the fall of the satellites was the catalyst, but the problems we face now? They're a whole lot bigger than communication and GPS."

Which was something that Liam had chewed on long and hard since June 6th. You had to fully understand the problem before you could come up with a solution, and right now... Even if every satellite they'd ever had suddenly worked again, they would still be facing some very big problems.

"Anything else you want to see?" Stan asked.

"Yeah, take me to the person who makes the duty roster."

He would stay, unless Cade or Harper found something profoundly disturbing. He'd stay, and he'd speak with Jackson Castillo. That conversation could very well determine the future, not just of Liam, Cade, and Harper, not just of the children, but of the entire population of Alpine.

Chapter 23

H ARPER HEADED TOWARD THE daycare first. Her arm was still healing, but it felt good to stretch her legs. Olivia skipped along beside her. The little girl looked relaxed for the first time since Harper had seen her on the top of Guadalupe Mountain.

It was amazing how resilient children were.

How they bounced back.

Olivia had seen her mother shot, spent several nights on a mountain with only her brother to look out for her, and then watched her mother die. Yet here she was, skipping down the middle of the road next to Harper.

Which reminded her of a trip she'd taken to Mackinac Island years before. It had been such a relief to walk down the middle of the road, to not worry about cars, to not see or hear or smell traffic. "Be careful what you wish for," she muttered to herself.

It was easy enough to find the childcare center. The kids were outside running around the playground. An older woman was monitoring the activity. She waved at Harper, but didn't approach. Instead, she allowed Harper to stand there and drink in the sight of children, playing outside, on a beautiful October morning. For those few minutes, Olivia stuck close to Harper's side, but soon the allure of other children won.

"Promise you won't leave me?"

"I promise."

Olivia pushed her favorite doll—the oldest, dirtiest one—into Harper's hands. "Hold this, please." And then she took off across the playground.

Harper walked over to the woman, who looked to be in her late fifties or early sixties. She was dressed in jeans and a t-shirt that read—

Best Grandma Ever

"Your daughter is adorable."

Harper smiled and didn't correct her. Instead, she held out her hand. "I'm Harper Moore."

"You came in a few days ago...with a bullet in your arm." The woman smiled broadly. "Word gets around in Alpine. I'm Sandra Mullins. My husband, Ron, is—well, he was—the Director of Public Works."

"He's on the council."

"He is." She smiled then nodded toward a bench. "Care to sit?"

"Sure."

They watched the children for a few minutes. Finally Harper said, "I have a few questions."

"I thought you might."

"Why a daycare?"

"Ah."

"Don't get me wrong. It's amazing to see something like this after June 6th."

Sandra smiled understandingly. "We've called it everything from *The Fall* to *The Cascade* and half a dozen other names in between. Now we've settled on saying *since June*, and everyone knows what you mean."

"And the daycare?"

"Everyone needs to work—every adult and every teenager for that matter. It's hard to do that if you're toting a three-year-old around. My daughter is one of the nurses working under Doc Turner, and my son-in-law rides the perimeter. They needed my help."

She pointed out a girl who looked to be a year younger than Olivia and a boy who was probably four. "Those are my grands. I love them more than the air that I breathe. I could keep them at my house, of course, but this way we're able to provide childcare for anyone who needs it."

"You have help, I assume."

"I do." Sandra smiled. "*The Grandmas*...that's what we call the early group ...are here from seven in the morning until noon. After that, we switch off with some of the teenagers—boys and girls."

"The teens work here?"

"Every Alpine high school student attends classes in the morning and performs some sort of work in the afternoon. Some work in the community garden, some help at the clinic where they learn medical skills, others work with the horses. They decide what they're interested in learning, and we make it happen."

"An apprenticeship."

"Pretty much."

"Wow."

"It's not perfect. Teens are still teens, and they can get easily distracted. We always have an adult overseeing them. But after the Marfa Battle, everyone seemed to understand the seriousness of the situation."

"Tell me about that. The Marfa Battle."

Sandra did, in clear, concise, unemotional language. But her eyes reflected how difficult those days had been. Finding the body of their former mayor. Learning that a woman named Regina, one of Tanda's officers, had switched sides. Being under attack by a group of Marfa residents who had combined with other stragglers.

The attempt to steal their supplies.

The shoot-outs and the deaths that followed.

Burying their dead.

Finding that others had left in the middle of the night.

"Why would they do that?"

"In some cases, we don't know why. In other cases, they left notes. Some felt that they made less of a target if they were on their own. Some hoped things would be better elsewhere."

"Things aren't better in El Paso. I can tell you that."

Sandra nodded, as if she'd expected as much. "Ron said the council approved your group to stay."

"They did."

"Will you?"

"I don't know," Harper answered honestly. "I'd like to, but I can't afford to do something because it sounds good. I have to do what's best for Olivia and her brother Jack."

"And your little one."

"Yes." Harper pressed a hand to the right side of her stomach, where she imagined the baby sleeping.

"If you ask my opinion, which you haven't, Alpine is a good place to ride this out. Whether it lasts another month or ten more years."

From what Harper had seen and experienced ten years sounded like an optimistic timetable. Another month sounded impossible.

"You seem like a good person," Sandra added. "We need as much help here as we can get. Plus, there's strength in numbers."

"As long as you can trust the people you're with."

"Exactly. As my husband is fond of quoting, *trust is the coin of the realm.*"

"I like that."

"Thank you, but I didn't come up with it. That's a quote by George Shultz."

"I'm not familiar with that name."

Sandra smiled, patted Harper's hand, and stood. "Nixon administration, which was well before your time."

When Sandra called the children inside, Harper tagged along, Olivia once again at her side. The Grandmas had set out snacks of canned peaches, graham crackers, and milk.

"Where does the milk come from?"

"Nubian goats. Stick around long enough and you'll find yourself raising a few."

Olivia was invited to share the snack. She looked to Harper for permission, then squeezed into line next to Sandra's granddaughter.

After she'd eaten, they walked to the middle school. The principal, a black man named Ezekiel Carter with hair turned white, offered to give her the nickel tour. They viewed a few classes as Olivia sat in the office coloring.

"Our numbers are low," Carter explained. "We decided the best use of our resources...we're short of nearly everything...was to combine two grades together—first and second, third and fourth, etc. We find it's actually helped their learning."

Harper had explained a little of her background and what she did before June 6th. Watching the fourth graders help the third graders with their math, she said, "I wrote a book years ago that had an Amish angle to it. I remember being surprised by how successful their one-room schoolhouses were."

"Doesn't surprise me. What with national and state regulations, we'd moved pretty far away from our primary job, which is to teach reading and writing. Preparing young men and women for the world."

It was hard not to like Ezekiel Carter. He had a smile that dazzled, and it was plain that the students adored and respected him.

"Any student problems?"

"Some. Attendance isn't mandatory at this point. That might be understandable if your parents are bringing in a crop, but if the kid's just sitting home sleeping the day away, it's not healthy."

"What do you do in that case?"

"Intercede the best we can."

They made their way back to the office where Harper collected Olivia. She thanked Ezekiel Carter for the tour.

He nodded thoughtfully and said, "We could use your expertise here. The ability to tell a story and to accurately reflect the world around you...that's a skill I would hate to see lost by the next generation."

Harper wanted to check out the food supply situation, but Olivia was plainly exhausted, and Harper's right arm was beginning to throb. "How about we head back to the gym and take a nap?"

Olivia yawned broadly, then said, "But I'm not tired, Harper."

"Let's do it for me then."

"Okay. I might not sleep, but I'll keep you company."

They both were passed out within five minutes of lying down. Harper dreamed of her first college writing class, which in the dream was interrupted by

Nubian goats climbing on the desks and nibbling on the books. She was walking between the desks, trying to shoo the goats to the floor when she looked up and stared out the classroom window. On the horizon were black clouds that filled the sky and brought with them a sense of foreboding.

Chapter 24

C ADE HAD NO TROUBLE finding Miles Turner's office. His waiting room was full, but his assistant, a woman who introduced herself as Anita Sanchez, seemed to have no problem keeping everything and everyone in order.

Miles worked through the backlog of patients efficiently and with compassion. Cade noticed that he had two nurses assisting him. When the last of the patients left, Miles told Anita, "I'm taking Doctor Dawson over to Cameron's."

"Bring me back some of his soup?"

"I'll do it if you'll let me leave Zeus."

Anita stared down at the dog asleep under her desk. "Deal."

They walked down the block and turned the corner. "There's a restaurant?" Cade asked in disbelief.

"Oh, there is a restaurant. You, my friend, are in for a treat."

Half of the tables were full and the smell coming from the back of the kitchen caused Cade's stomach to grumble.

"I can't believe you have a restaurant."

"Sweet, right?"

The chef came out to personally tell them what was on the menu. "Squash soup with seasoned crackers, quail stuffed with jalapenos and served with wild rice, or chicken pot pie."

"Seriously?"

The chef was built like a linebacker and looked as if he'd stepped off a movie set. He smiled widely and shook his head, saying in an aside to Miles, "New guys. They're always surprised we can still cook."

"I'm surprised you have anything to cook."

"Ah." He stuck out his hand. "Name's Cameron Boyd, and I think you're going to love what we're able to rustle up here in Alpine."

"Cade Dawson, and as you figured out, I'm new."

"Good to meet you. Since Doc brought you in, I don't even need a voucher. Now what'll it be?"

Cade ordered the quail and Miles asked for the chicken. When they once again had the table to themselves, Cade asked, "What gives? I feel like I've stepped into the past. What's a voucher?"

Miles sat forward, holding his cup of water and staring into it. Finally he sat back and settled that unwavering gaze on Cade. "People need more than food, medical care, school. They need something to look forward to. Something to break the monotony of a life that has grown inexplicably hard."

"So you created vouchers?"

"Don't say it that way. We couldn't think of another name for it."

"How do you get one?"

"Easy." He waved a hand toward the rest of the customers. "Work an extra shift, do something above and beyond, aim for excellence, have a birthday."

"Or be the town doctor."

"Yup."

"Where does the food come from?"

"People donate it. That, too, earns you a voucher."

"And Cameron? This is his job instead of riding the perimeter?"

"Trust me. When you taste Cameron's cooking, you'd be willing to take a perimeter shift for him."

A teenager bustled out with their food, served on plates with what looked like a sprig of parsley on the side. It was the first fresh green thing Cade had seen in months, and it was the first thing he popped in his mouth.

"I think that was decoration."

"And yet I ate it."

They laughed and tucked in to their food.

Cade had eaten in Houston's most expensive restaurants, but he'd never tasted anything better. As they ate, Miles explained about the medical practice, the apprenticeship for nurses and doctors, as well as the status of their medical supplies.

"It was a big loss when the medical center burned down. We salvaged what we could, but..." He shook his head, then pushed away his empty plate.

"The thing you've done with blood transfusions is pretty amazing."

"Thank you."

"No, seriously. You saved Harper's life."

Miles nodded, his eyes saying that he understood. Maybe he did. "My biggest concern is medication. We simply don't have enough. Most of my patients who were on any type of critical medication have died."

"If you could have anything?"

"Antibiotics."

Cade understood. He'd struggled with that in El Paso as well.

"We've found some natural substitutes, but it's not enough."

"Will you send out scavenger parties?"

"Interesting name."

"It's what we called them in El Paso."

"The problem here in far west Texas is that it's a long way between towns. We will send out parties. We'll have to, but it will be carefully and meticulously planned."

They thanked their server, and Miles asked him to send some soup over to the medical office. Then they walked out onto the nearly deserted downtown street. "We have trade days here every Saturday. People bring what they no longer need and trade it for something they want. You'd be surprised how well it works. You can get everything from goat milk to eggs to a newly knitted sweater."

"What is the food situation?"

"Stable for now." Miles explained about the hunting parties, the shared meat, how every family planted a garden. "Most also have Nubian goats for milk. We were fortunate that there was a farm outside of town. Krissy and Mike Scott were willing to share what they knew, teach others how to raise the animals, and they had enough stock to breed more."

"Every home has a goat?"

"Pretty much. Milk and fresh vegetables, they've been more critical than meat. I'm concerned about carbs. We aren't able to grow enough vegetables to put much back for winter, and the few supplies we have will be gone by next year."

"You'll need those scavenger parties."

"Maybe, in the interim. But the long-term solution, if we're talking long-te rm..."

Cade nodded. That was what he needed to know. What was Alpine doing to prepare for next year and the year after that? Because it did no good to settle his family in a town that they'd have to leave in another six months. He did not want to be on the road with a newborn infant.

With his newborn infant.

"Trade routes. Texas has a wide diversity of crops. Rice in the southeast. Citrus in the Rio Grande Valley. The problem is everything is so damn far away. We need to establish trade routes"

They walked a few more minutes, then stopped and sat at a patio table outside what had once been a wine bar.

"I'm guessing you have questions."

"A few."

Miles raised his hand and motioned toward himself. Everything from his posture to his smile said, *Give 'em to me.*

"Why are you the only doctor here?"

"Don't forget Logan."

"Okay. Why are you two the only doctors here?"

"Most of the Alpine physicians were out of town at a convention on June 6th. Short-sighted of them I know, but few people really believed something of this magnitude could happen. The town's only remaining physician, Doc Fielder, died of a heart attack within the first few days. That's when Tanda appeared on my doorstep."

"I don't understand. You weren't practicing here before June 6th?"

"Nope. I'd bought a cabin outside of town. I was hunkered down. Hiding, if you want to know the truth."

"Hiding from what?"

"Grief."

Cade didn't know how to answer that. He simply stared at the man and waited.

"I was living, and practicing medicine, in Houston when my wife and daughter were killed in a random shooting. I stayed long enough to see the person responsible convicted, and then I came out here. To hide, I suppose. Or maybe to heal."

"And Tanda found you?"

"Well first Zeus found me, and after that Tanda did."

"Wow. I'm sorry that happened to you. I'm sorry for your loss, Miles, and I sincerely mean that. I can't imagine what I would do if I lost Harper."

Miles nodded. "Alpine grows on you. Maybe it's the fact that it's so far west. The people are tough."

"I saw some of that in El Paso too. It seemed to me that we didn't know how tough we were until our survival depended on it."

"Exactly. We could use you here, Cade. If I were speaking frankly, I'd say you could make the difference between Alpine surviving or not."

"No pressure..."

"No pressure." Miles laughed lightly, a chuckle really, but it lightened the man's expression. "I can train nurses and assistants, but I can't train another doctor who has your experience."

"I understand that. Leaving El Paso wasn't an easy decision. I did it because of Harper." *And Tía* he thought, but he didn't go into that. "I need to know that Alpine is a good place, a safe place. If that even exists anymore."

"I can't guarantee you it's safe. Any man who does, I suggest you walk away. But I can tell you that we're pulling together here. We will stand, or fall, together."

Those words stayed with Cade as he walked the streets of Alpine and finally returned to the gymnasium.

He and Harper and Liam met again that evening after the children were asleep. They pulled their chairs into a circle and voted, and the vote was unanimous.

They would stay in Alpine.

Chapter 25

Harper, Cade, Jack, and Olivia were given the use of an older bungalow-style home on the northwest side of town. It had three bedrooms and one bath, though there was no running water. The people who owned it had been caught out of town.

"Of course, if they return, you'll have to relocate." Akule Lopez, Tanda's niece, handed them a set of keys. "Most people don't lock their doors. Kinda what's the point, and anyone who is the bad sort is gone."

"You don't have any crime here?" Harper had been studying the kitchen. She hadn't believed she'd ever have a kitchen again. Was it less than a month ago that she'd been living in a bus with Cade? Now she had two additional children...and a kitchen.

"We have some crime," Akule admitted. "Consists mainly of people getting rowdy, blowing off steam. A few fights now and then."

"What do you do?"

"One night in a jail cell tends to cool them off, if that's even necessary. Most people, though, they're too tired at the end of the day to get into trouble."

"Thank you, Akule." Cade shook her hand.

She looked embarrassed, but returned the handshake.

"Guess I'll be seeing you at the university," she said to Harper, and then she was gone.

"Nice kid," Harper noted.

"Kid? Akule?"

"She turns twenty-one next week. I call that a kid."

He pulled her into his arms, and they stood there a minute. She was suddenly and fully aware of the press of her belly against Cade's stomach—of the child growing within her. It was perhaps the first time since she'd made her way to the northern barrio of El Paso that she'd felt at ease.

Maybe that was a good thing, maybe it wasn't.

Getting too comfortable could be dangerous.

"How did Tía know?" She murmured against Cade's chest.

He didn't even try to answer her, and that was one of the things she loved about him. Sometimes he just let her questions be.

The moment of quiet was broken by Jack and Olivia dashing into the room. "There's so much stuff here." Jack was holding a baseball in one hand, a novel in the other hand. "Are you sure it's okay for us to use it?"

"My room has dolls." Olivia hadn't brought them out with her. She continued to clutch the old ones that had been rescued from their camper.

Harper experienced a sharp ache in her heart at the look of confusion on their faces. She walked over to the kitchen table, pulled out a chair, sat, and waved them over. "Let's have our first family meeting."

Jack's expression remained grave.

Olivia simply shrugged and followed her brother.

"We've been given this house to use. If the people who own it come back, then we'll move to a different house." Cade waited for questions, but Jack and Olivia continued to watch them silently.

Harper cleared her throat. "We've been invited to stay here in Alpine."

"For how long?" Jack's expression was now screwed into a scowl.

"As long as we want to." Cade crossed his arms on the table and waited.

"Oh," Jack said.

Olivia stared at her dolls, then looked from Cade to Harper. "So I can sleep in that room? The one with dolls?"

"You sure can," Harper said. "And you can play with the toys."

Jack still wasn't convinced. He looked so impossibly young to Harper. How was it that this child had been made to suffer so much? How was it that he had come out of that suffering with his sense of right and wrong still intact?

"How do we know that they would want us to? I mean, it's someone else's stuff. All of this, is someone else's stuff."

Cade looked up at the ceiling a minute, then he tapped the table. "Tell me about your home, back in Dallas."

"Well, it was a little newer than this. We had a computer in the living room on this small desk, and we could play on it if our chores and homework were done." He glanced down at the baseball and glove in his hands. "I was starting a baseball card collection. My dad was showing me how."

"Okay. Excellent. So if some family found your old home, and they needed a place to stay, how would you feel about that?"

"I wouldn't mind," Jack answered immediately. "Someone should be using that stuff."

"Great. That's a good answer, and I suspect the boy and girl, mom and dad who lived here wouldn't mind our using their stuff."

"Because we'll be careful with it."

"Of course we will," Harper agreed.

"I'll take real good care of the dolls," Olivia chimed in, and a smile broke through her usually somber expression. It didn't last, though. "I miss Mommy."

"And Dad," Jack said softly.

"We all have people we miss," Harper said. "That's okay. It's okay to be sad and to wish they were here."

Jack nodded and swiped at his eyes with the back of his hand.

Olivia slid out from her chair, walked over to Harper and climbed up into her lap. Her face pressed against Harper's chest. Her voice was a whisper that filled the room with all of her nightmares and all of her dreams.

"Harper, do we get to stay with you, like, forever?"

"Yeah." She kissed the top of Olivia's head, brushed her hair out of her eyes, blinked back her tears, and smiled at Jack. "Exactly like forever."

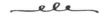

It was the next day that she made it over to Sul Ross. Akule had left a note on the kitchen counter, telling her to go to the third floor of the Academic Building—the same building they had been interviewed in. Harper wasn't sure what she expected to see when she got there.

Stacks of spiral-bound notebooks and pens?

A chisel and a rock?

Instead, she hiked up the stairs to the third floor, rounded the corner, and came across what looked very much like a library. Sunlight streamed through floor-to-ceiling windows. Tables had been set up with writing stations in the center of the room. Each held a lamp, a pad of paper and pen for taking notes, and a laptop computer.

Students were typing on laptop computers.

A woman who looked to be in her forties stood and walked toward her. She was tall and willowy, with raven black hair and pronounced cheekbones.

"Peggy Looper." She offered a firm handshake. "And you must be Harper."

"Yes. I am."

Peggy smiled at her. "I've read some of your books. I enjoyed them immensely."

"Thank you." Harper didn't know what else to say. She felt as if she'd stepped into an alternate universe—perhaps the one she had inhabited before June 6th.

"During the school year it was all textbooks, literary classics, and student papers, but on summer break...on summer break I read whatever my heart desired."

And with those words, the spell was broken. Peggy Looper struck Harper as being about as real and authentic and unpretentious as a person could be. Peggy Looper struck her as someone that she would enjoy working with.

"We're calling this the Legacy Project."

"Good name."

"The goal is to keep a written record of the days since June 6th.

"Explain to me about the computers."

"They're solar charged, which is why we picked this room. When a computer is not in use, it's hooked up to a charger." Peggy walked her over to the window sills. Each had a solar charger affixed to the ledge. Beneath the ledge was a shelf. "Computers go on the shelf. We're not sure that prolonged sunlight will hurt them, but why take a chance?"

"So basically, these are dummy terminals."

"Correct, because they aren't connected to a cloud of any sort," Peggy smiled, and it was as if a light from within was shining through. "The WiFi does still work."

"But there's nothing to connect to."

"Correct. Nothing *out there* to connect to." She waved a hand toward the windows. "We can still send files to each other, and we can connect to the printers."

"You have printers." The words came out softly, filled with wonder.

"We do, and they work! The challenge we face is supplies—paper and toner. We only print the final versions. Then we backup to a zip drive, which we deliver to Tanda once a week."

"What does she do with it?"

"Stores it somewhere safe."

"It isn't safe here?"

Peggy shrugged. "We like to think we are. In truth, if Alpine were overrun, they would find our supplies—all of our supplies. Who knows what they would do with this. Steal it, maybe. Or destroy it, simply because they can."

Harper thought of the Watchmen and nodded. People were reacting to the changing world differently. For some that included violence and destruction.

"We keep a print copy and an additional digital copy here, plus what is on the devices. We'd like to have another print copy to give Tanda, but at this point, I'm not comfortable using what supplies we have for backups of our backups."

They'd reach a sitting area of sorts. Eight oversized chairs like you might find in a living room were pulled into a sort of circle. Coffee tables and night stands were spaced at intervals between the chairs.

"We hold our meetings here." Peggy perched on the edge of one of the chairs. "I can see you have questions."

Harper sat across from her, trying to corral her thoughts into something coherent. "I guess the biggest question I have is...what's the point?"

Peggy didn't answer immediately. She studied the ceiling a moment, then let her gaze drift around the room. Finally, she turned her attention to Harper. "In my mind, there are two."

She ticked the first off on her index finger. "A written history is what separates us from Neanderthals, though even they tried to leave a lasting mark that they had existed."

"Cave drawings."

"In particular the Chauvet Cave in France and the Cave of Altamira in Spain. We can only guess at what those drawings mean since written language wasn't developed at that point. But we do have written language, and we should use it. Leaving a record of what we think happened, and of the days and years after the event, isn't just important. It's integral to our very nature of what it means to be human."

Harper nodded in agreement. "And the second reason?"

Peggy used her finger to trace the inside of her palm. "It's my opinion that we use writing to make sense of the world around us. Many teenagers keep a journal. Many adults, before the cascade, dreamed of writing a book."

"Some people wrote music. Others painted."

"And if you walk through our art district, you'll see that they still do." She tapped the arm of the chair she was sitting in.

It was covered with a rose chintz fabric which struck Harper as impossibly extravagant. Had someone picked it because it matched the color of the walls? Had such things once really mattered?

"Many of the people here are working on the Legacy Project, but others come in because they need to write about what has happened to them, they need to voice their personal story."

"Their stories could be part of the Project."

"True, but sometimes they prefer to keep them private. My point is this floor is open to everyone, though we save the printing supplies for the Legacy Project." She laughed. "Edna Banks works at the police station. Has for years.

She'll come in after work and use one of the computers. When she has what she's working on just right, she'll copy it down on to paper. I asked her once why she was doing it that way...rather backwards from what we'd normally do. Do you know what she said?"

Harper shook her head.

"She said that she understood paper had become a rare and precious commodity. She could type on the computers, edit and re-edit what she wanted to say, then write it out once she was satisfied with the final product."

"What does she write about?"

Peggy stood and smoothed her blouse. "Poetry, Harper. She writes poetry."

Chapter 26

I T TOOK FOUR DAYS before Liam found himself alone with Jackson. It was pitch dark, and they were riding the northwest perimeter of Alpine on horseback. Strange what you could become used to. The horse had a smooth gait, and Liam found he didn't miss the jeep or walking. The pace that Jackson set was perfect—fast enough to cover ground, slow enough to pay attention to everything.

The first few miles of their patrol, the kid Dylan rode with him. Then Logan Wright called him on the radio. "I'm having trouble with a heifer. The calf's turned. I could use another set of hands."

"I'm on my way," Dylan replied with a broad smile. He tossed the radio to Jackson, nodded at Liam, and galloped back toward town.

"That boy loves any excuse to run a horse rather than walk it."

"Did he grow up here?"

"He did. Rodeo star, football hero, and major fool before June 6th. Somehow he came out of this thing better and brighter."

They walked their horses west, watching for anything that didn't belong.

It was quiet.

They were alone.

Liam understood this was his chance. "How long have you been with E unit?"

Jackson grunted. "Since before you were born. You?"

"Eight years." Over the years, he'd heard various explanations for the name of this specialized unit that included all branches of the military.

Exceptional because they were supposedly the best.

Extraordinary because the things they were asked to do went above and beyond.

Essential. When he'd been approached, the general who spoke to him had used that word. "What we're doing here, what we're preparing for—God forbid that we ever need it—will be essential."

He'd slowly embraced the opinion that what the E stood for didn't matter. If you joined up, you joined up forever. Like the tattooed symbol on the inside of his wrist and Jackson's wrist—it was something that you carried with you long after your military service ended.

It was something you carried to your grave.

"You're E1."

"I am which means I'm a damn sight older than you."

"Have you been contacted, since June 6th?"

"I have not, though it occurred to me that might be why you're here."

Liam shook his head, then realized that Jackson probably couldn't see that, so he said, "No."

Jackson stopped his horse as they reached a rise. There wasn't a lot to see—most was darkness in the distance. There were the stars, the barest sliver of moon, and under all of that the people of Alpine, the Watchmen, and possibly their commanding officer.

Liam asked, "Do you have one of the new control boxes?"

"I do."

"Have you used it?"

"I have not."

"Should we use it now?"

"I don't know." Then Jackson added unnecessarily, "We only get one chance..."

"The Watchmen probed the east side last night. They're coming, and we need to be prepared for them."

"Being prepared isn't enough," Jackson pointed out. "Being prepared is a defensive posture. What we need is to be on the offense."

"How do we do that?"

"We talk to Tanda."

They didn't speak of it again, but the next evening when Liam reported for his patrol duty he was handed a note signed with Tanda's signature. It read simply, "My office—now."

Dylan shrugged. "She's a hard-ass, but she's also a good boss. I'd get there pronto, amigo."

Liam walked into the office to find the place empty other than Tanda and Jackson.

"Don't you usually keep an officer at the front desk?" Liam asked.

"I sent Makowski home early. Told him I'd cover the shift."

"Okay."

"Jackson said that there's something you both need to talk to me about. So, let's hear it."

Her face was devoid of expression. Perhaps that was her Native American heritage, or maybe she'd learned not to give away what she was thinking. She was small, not even five and a half feet, maybe 130 pounds, with long straight black hair that he'd only seen pulled back in a band. Her eyes were a dark brown and seemed to be assessing everything, all the time.

Jackson had been silent up to this point. He'd removed the Stetson that he wore everywhere. His skin looked as worn as the saddles on their horses. His expression was almost relieved. He'd been carrying the burden of the E Unit alone for a long time.

"Okay. Well, I don't know what Jackson has told you."

"Nothing."

"Okay. Jackson and I are both part of something called the E Unit."

"Wait...you knew each other? From before?"

"No. Not at all." Liam pulled up the sleeve of his shirt to reveal his tattoo, an E18.

Jackson did the same, E1.

Instead of reacting, Tanda rotated her hand, indicating he should continue.

"The E Unit consists of service members—"

"From what branch?"

"All branches."

She nodded.

"Those service members are sometimes approached by their commanding officer. They're told the bare bones about the unit—"

"Which is?"

"That we're to constitute a last line of defense against civilian revolts. If you agree to join, it's a permanent assignment."

"Permanent?"

"It's forever," Jackson explained. "Even when you leave the military, you're still a part of the E Unit."

Tanda thought about that a minute, then nodded. "Sort of like there's no such thing as an ex-Marine."

"Exactly." Liam had expected Jackson to take point on this, but the old guy seemed content to let Liam stumble through it. "That's why I was tracking Cade. My assignment was to find those persons deemed necessary for the continuance of a functioning society."

"But that changed at Guadalupe Peak. Your dedication to that cause changed when you saw the tent city and heard about the murder of Ashley."

"Yes. And no." He shifted in his seat, suddenly wishing that he were standing—feet shoulder-width apart, posture perfect, hands clasped behind his back. But he wasn't standing at attention in front of his CO. He was sitting in a rather comfortable chair in a room lit by a gas lantern as the last rays of light disappeared from the sky outside.

He was debriefing a small-town police chief in an apocalyptic world.

"I'm still assigned to the E Unit. I always will be, but I now believe that the command structure of my branch of that unit was corrupted."

Tanda sighed and sat back. She steepled her fingers and stared at him. Finally, she asked, "Why are you telling me this?"

Instead of answering, he reached for his backpack, unzipped it, and pulled out the box that he'd kept hidden there since leaving the northern barrio. Jackson reached into a leather saddle bag and did the same. They placed both on Tanda's desk.

The boxes were approximately eight inches by five, made of a nanotechnology that would allow them to be opened only by the palmprint of the person it was assigned to. Nothing else would open it. You could drop a sledgehammer on it and there would be no sign of impact.

"What are those?"

"They're a tool, given to us to use at our discretion and only in the most extreme of situations."

"This is an extreme situation?"

Jackson bristled. "The Watchmen are coming, Tanda. We don't know how many. We don't know what supplies they have. We don't know how to defend against them. Yes, it's an extreme situation."

"All right. Show me what's in there."

Liam glanced at Jackson, who nodded once. Liam reached forward and grasped the box with his left palm—they always keyed it to your less dominant hand. The box easily opened. He stared at its contents for a several seconds, then he pushed it across Tanda's desk.

She studied it, said nothing, and then nodded for him to take it back.

"Will they know it's been opened?"

"No. An alert is only sent when it's activated."

"And how long will we have after that?"

"Depends who's in charge."

"And it will allow us to..." She raised a finger toward the sky and circled it.

"Yeah."

Tanda stood. Jackson and Liam immediately did the same. She hadn't looked surprised, which was odd. Maybe she'd reached that place where nothing surprised her anymore.

Or maybe she was very good at hiding her reactions.

Either way, Liam understood why she was the duly elected leader of Alpine. Her title didn't matter nearly as much as the fact that she was unflappable, decisive, and trusted.

She walked them out of her office, pushed open the door to the police station, and waited until they'd walked through. "Admin building at eight tonight."

Then she turned and walked back into the police station, and it seemed to Liam that she was carrying a burden that no single person should be made to bear.

Chapter 27

C ADE WAS SURPRISED TO be summoned to the Admin Building, but he didn't even consider ignoring the sheet of paper that had been delivered to him.

"I'll tell you everything," he promised as he kissed Harper.

"You'd better. I'm on the Legacy Project, you know. All this has to be documented—even our secrets." She was smiling, but behind that smile was a seriousness that he'd come to associate with Harper. She was constantly thinking things through, exploring options, repercussions, possible outcomes.

"Legacy Project. Need to know. Got it."

Jack and Olivia were already in their pajamas. They'd eaten dinner, gone over homework, and had their baths. The image before him as he left that night was one from the past—one of a normal life, of a life that he didn't believe still existed.

And maybe it didn't.

Maybe what he was seeing was a mirage.

He arrived at the Admin Building after a twenty-minute walk and found a small group.

Tanda, Miles, and Logan.

Jackson and Liam.

Keme.

Instead of the middle of the room, they'd pulled the chairs over to the windows and formed a tight circle. Two black boxes had been placed on the table in the middle of the chairs.

Tanda didn't waste any time getting started. "We're meeting because we may have a one-time opportunity to stop the Watchmen. Liam and Jackson came to me this morning to explain their *situation*—"

She hesitated on that word, then pushed on. "I stopped them as soon as I realized what they were saying was something you all needed to hear."

"Why us?" Keme asked.

Tanda sighed. "I can't do this alone. I won't. It's our responsibility to lead."

One veterinarian, two doctors, a police chief, one rancher, one former military, and one Native American liaison. Cade thought it was an oddly patched-together form of leadership, but his instinct said to trust Tanda's assessment.

"And the others?" Miles asked.

"I'll brief them, but it's been a difficult few nights with the Watchmen testing our perimeter. We had another fence cut and some supplies stolen on the west side. Nothing we can't live without, but I still have the sense that they're planning something bigger. Gonzo and Ron are on patrol tonight. Dixie and Emmanuel are off. They need that time."

"I agree." Logan sat back, crossed his arms. "So, spill it. What's in the boxes?"

Cade knew very little about advanced technology or governmental programs...maybe as much as the average American did before June 6th.

Maybe less.

Most of his waking hours had been dedicated to medicine. Any free time he'd had was spent catching up on sleep or riding his Ducati Monster through the area surrounding El Paso. He'd bought the iconic motorcycle and rebuilt it. That motorcycle had saved his life at a time when he thought what was expected of him on a daily basis was more than he had to give.

He couldn't have even imagined what would be expected of him after June 6th.

Liam explained about something called the E Unit, how both he and Jackson were members though they'd never met before, what the purpose of the unit was, and how he felt the command structure of his unit had been corrupted.

"What about yours, Jackson?" Miles was leaning forward, elbows on his knees, hands intertwined.

"I haven't heard from my unit," Jackson admitted. "Boxes like this one would arrive, and my directions were to send the previous one back. They always included the latest technology. Within twenty-four hours of delivery, I'd receive an encrypted email with instructions on how to use it."

"Did you ever use those previous boxes?"

"No. There was never a reason to."

"Okay." Miles turned to Liam. "What about you? Have you ever used the technology in the boxes?"

"I have, but then remember I'm still technically in the military. Occasionally I'd be called away from my regular unit to attend to E Unit business. That usually included being trained in whatever the latest gadget was."

Cade noticed that Keme hadn't spoken at all. He actually wasn't responding in anyway, though he was intensely present—an odd way to describe a person but apt in this case.

Logan picked up the questions where Miles had left off. "You think this can help us?"

When both Liam and Jackson nodded, Logan continued. "We have a problem with the Watchmen, so you two broke your vow of silence."

"It wasn't a vow exactly." Liam tried to get comfortable in his seat. "But yeah."

"You both believe that what's in those boxes will help us deal with our current situation."

"Yes," they answered simultaneously.

Liam sat up straighter.

Jackson stared at the window.

Cade wondered how much courage it had taken to step forward. They had to know that admitting their allegiance was somewhere else, outside of Alpine, could mean their being ostracized. They had to know that from this moment forward, there wasn't any turning back.

But that could be true for all of them, he supposed.

He would never ride his Ducati again, never walk onto a fully staffed hospital floor. Life had changed. It was as simple and true a fact as the rising and setting of the sun.

"Let's see it then." Logan sat back, hands clasped behind his head. "You have my attention."

Liam and Jackson each picked up his box and palmed it with his left hand. The boxes opened. Everyone in the group leaned forward, everyone except Tanda, who had apparently already had a look. Inside each box was what looked like a fly, a glove, and a device approximately the size of a smart phone.

It was Keme who broke the silence. "Nano technology?"

"Yes."

"The box as well as the spybot, controller, and monitor?"

"Yes."

"Wait. That's a spybot?" Cade shook his head, trying to catch up with whatever Keme had already surmised. "Are you kidding? There's a camera in that?"

Keme was the one to answer. "Richard Guiler and Tom Vaneck first conceived the idea of insect drones over ten years ago. By 2011, AeroVironment had developed a Nano Hummingbird. It weighed only nineteen grams, but it carried a camera, communication systems, and an energy system."

"Correct on all accounts," Liam said. "We control its path with the glove, and we're able to see what it sees with the monitor."

"Wow." Logan sat back. "You're way out of my field of expertise. I just fix animals."

"And people," Miles corrected, high-fiving his friend.

It was so ridiculous, so much like what two teenagers would do, that Cade laughed and shook his head. "I feel like I'm in an episode of *The Twilight Zone*," he admitted.

Tanda's right eyebrow arched, and she almost smiled. "What we're here to do is assess the risks and then determine if moving forward with these devices is wise."

"Okay. What are the drawbacks?" Miles asked.

"Once you key in a destination, it's tracked," Keme said.

Liam nodded. "Right. Now, we don't know that anyone on the other end is watching. We have no idea how many personnel the E Unit lost on June 6th. They could be dealing with much bigger things than a spybot in the desert."

"Could be," Keme sat back, crossed his arms. "They still work because they're connected to a satellite in the upper orbit?"

"Right again. As stated in my last debriefing, which was six weeks ago, those satellites were unaffected."

"Meaning what?" Tanda stood and began pacing. "Does it mean that eventually the world will return to normal?"

"No." Jackson's answer was firm, unyielding.

Tanda dropped back into her chair.

"Look. If I can understand it, then it's not that complicated." Liam picked up an empty soft drink can that had been left on one of the tables and smooshed it flat. "Pretend this is Earth. Most commercial satellites were placed in LEO—lower Earth orbit."

"Too many, apparently." Logan shrugged. "That's what the scientists at the observatory told us. Kessler Effect and all that."

"Exactly. All parties involved understood what *could* happen, but no one wanted to believe it *would* happen. No one seriously listened to Kessler."

"Except maybe someone did." The frown on Tanda's face eased up just a little.

"Yeah. The government understood that medium Earth orbit and geostationary orbit were the sweet spots, and that's where they placed the most critical satellites."

"Why not put everything up there?" Cade tried to envision men sitting in Washington D.C. and making these decisions. Decisions that affected the fate of a nation, of a world.

"Costs more. Takes more fuel to put them in orbit. And remember, lower earth satellites have an average speed of eight kilometer per second. Satellites in a geostationary orbit have an average speed of three kilometers per second. This is where most of the spy satellites are. Plus, since they're higher..." He held a hand above the soda can, fingers spread, palm down. "The coverage is wider...as much as forty-two percent."

"Wait." Cade held up a finger. "Geostationary...is that GPS?"

"It is."

"Then why doesn't GPS work?" Tanda asked. "The very first night, the night of the train collision, we had people stranded because their GPS wouldn't work."

"Yup. They didn't know how to follow the only road out of town." Logan smiled at Tanda and something—some history they shared—passed between them.

"The answer to whether GPS continued to work is both yes and no," Liam said. "The constellation arrangement run by the U.S. Space Force, which consists of thirty-one operational GPS satellites, was positioned in medium Earth orbit."

"So why did GPS stop working on our phones?" Logan asked. "Cars were still working, but not their nav systems."

"Your phones stopped working," Liam reminded him. "For whatever reason, and I am not a telecom specialist, they couldn't connect. The same was true of any car's navigation systems. The problem was on the user end."

"Okay. Let's pull this back," Tanda stood, walked over to a window, and stared out at the darkness. Finally, she turned back to the group. "Liam, you know how to operate the spybots."

"Yes," Liam said. "And I can train Jackson."

"Can you train him without activating it?"

"Yes. You can fly it in circles...hell, we could practice in Kokernot Field. When we turn on the nav system or the cameras, that's when we might attract the attention of our superiors."

"If they're watching."

"Right."

Tanda walked over to a backpack leaning against the wall and below the bank of windows. She unzipped the larger pocket and pulled out a map. Walking back to the circle of chairs, she unfolded the map and spread it across the table. She traced a finger from Alpine, following Highway 90, up to Van Horn.

Piercing Cade with a stare, she asked, "You were attacked here?"

"Correct. The entire town had been..." He shook his head, trying to dislodge the images that came to mind. "It had been trashed and marked by the Watchmen."

"Okay. Look at this." She hurried over to the backpack and pulled out a red marker, then began putting X's on the map. "These are the places where we think the Watchmen have tried to breach our perimeter."

"The bulk of the attacks have been on the west side," Jackson said.

"Correct, and the rest were on the north side." She grimaced. "Last night they managed to take two crates of MREs."

"They're hiding on the west side of Mount Livermore," Miles said.

"It's what this map seems to suggest."

"Unless they're trying to throw us off," Miles said.

"That would take more fuel than I think they'd waste."

"What about Marfa?" Cade asked, peering at the map.

"Didn't survive the June battle." Tanda sank onto the floor, studying the map. "We send out scouts. Keme, can a couple of your people head that way, without being seen?"

"They can, but if we're talking horses, that's at least a two-day ride."

"I say we use the fuel. Take a vehicle, travel at night, lights off. Any sign that you're getting close, park and reconnoiter on foot."

"Okay."

"Keme's men look for the encampment first. I don't want them getting close, though. They hang back and confirm where it is, how many people it includes, and what type of fire power they have."

"You got it."

"Once we're sure of the location, we take Jackson and Liam out. We'll only use one of the bots if we run into trouble."

"It would look less suspicious to use mine," Jackson said. "They don't know for certain that Liam is here."

"Right. If a commander traces it back to you, what would he do?"

"Maybe nothing. Maybe send someone down to find out what's happening."

"We'll deal with that if and when it occurs. Right now we have to stop the bleeding of our supplies by the Watchmen."

Tanda shook her head, and Cade was again aware of the weight that she was bearing on her shoulders, the weight of Alpine.

Her voice dropped to a near whisper, but it also held more certainty in it than he'd heard at the beginning of this meeting.

"Winter's coming. We take care of this problem now." Tanda glanced up, took in each person in the small group. "All in favor…"

Six hands went up. Tanda's expression lightened just a bit as she added her own, and Cade could have sworn that for the briefest of seconds she smiled. "It's decided. We locate and confront the Watchmen. Then we stop them—by whatever means is necessary."

Chapter 28

"WHY DID THEY INCLUDE you?" Harper asked. They were sleeping in a bed that wasn't theirs, and not a day went by that Harper didn't send a silent thank you to the family who had lived in this house before them.

Cade's laughter was soft, light, melodic. "I asked the same thing. Tanda said that Miles, Logan, and I constitute the entire medical community. She said that any decision made regarding the welfare of Alpine had to include us."

"Wow."

"Right?"

"I like her."

"Yup." Cade ran a finger over her still-bandaged arm. "We landed on our feet when we ended up here."

"That we did."

Harper had no doubt that they were both thinking of Tía. If they hadn't followed her advice, if they'd gone north instead of east...it didn't bear thinking about.

She fell asleep in the circle of his arms, and the next morning she embraced what she was thinking of as her new normal—getting Jack and Olivia ready for school, walking to the Sul Ross campus, losing herself in the pages of the Legacy Project. That afternoon, word came down regarding the Watchmen.

She was nibbling on her lunch when Peggy walked over and sat down beside her. "They found the encampment."

Harper didn't know whether she should be happy or worried about that pronouncement. It was necessary. She understood that. The wound on her arm was testament to that very fact.

"Where?"

"Where Tanda thought it would be. If you ask me, that woman has some of her ancestor's gift as far as intuition. An old encampment to the east of 90, but west of Mount Livermore."

"Okay. What do we do?"

"Town meeting later this afternoon. We'll both find out then."

Harper must have looked worried, because Peggy reached out and squeezed her hand. "It'll give me a chance to finally meet Jack and Olivia."

And the thought of those two children did what little else could, It gave Harper the faith and determination she would need to make it through one more thing. This post-modern life seemed to consist largely of getting through *One More Thing*. She always thought of those three words in capital letters, like the title of a chapter in the book of her life.

"Let's close up early so we can get down there in time."

Even the children had heard of the meeting. It seemed that Alpine had developed a communication grapevine that rivaled the cell phone network of yore. To Harper, it said much about the town that information was openly shared. When she'd mentioned as much to Cade, he'd said, "Makes sense though. It never did work to try to hide information from the people you were supposed to be serving."

It occurred to Harper that this was something she needed to add to the Legacy Project. How having so little had clarified ways they'd misused the luxury of having so much.

The meeting was held at a small gazebo.

Harper stood between Cade and Peggy, the children seated in front of them. She wasn't sure how many people she'd thought were in Alpine, but the crowd was both larger and smaller than what she'd envisioned. She knew from the Legacy Project that the population had been close to six thousand before June 6th. Some of those six thousand had been caught out of town, some had died because of medical complications, and some had died in the town's battle with Marfa. A few had quietly slipped away in the night, but that was happening less and less often.

Alpine was a good place to live, and that was evident in the faces around her. She'd put the number left at around eight hundred souls.

Fewer than she'd hoped for.

More than she'd feared.

The council plus Cade and Liam now sat on the steps of the gazebo. They looked for all the world like a group of friends about to share a picnic, when in fact they were there to lead the way. It was Tanda who stood to speak, and the crowd instantly quieted.

"We've located the Watchmen. They have a base north of Marfa, down an old ranch road that is west of Fort Davis."

"The hills of Mount Livermore," someone shouted back, and a light laughter drifted through the crowds.

Harper leaned toward Peggy. "What's the joke?"

"A few years ago, a developer showed up in town. They'd planned a huge timeshare resort and called it *The Hills of Mount Livermore.*"

"I'm guessing something went wrong."

Peggy smiled in a way that Harper was learning had a tinge of sadness as well as a splash of good humor. "They planned an eighteen-hole golf course, swimming pools, sculpted gardens—you should have seen the pamphlets. The problem was that they didn't account for the lack of water in the area. The development never happened, but the name stuck."

Tanda was reviewing how many times the Watchmen had struck and how much of Alpine's supplies they had stolen. "We're not in an emergency situation yet as far as winter supplies, but we don't want to end up in one either."

"We need to stop the bleeding sooner, not later." This from a white-haired woman sitting in a lawn chair at the front of the group.

"Our sentiments exactly, Mrs. Crowder." Tanda went on to explain that Liam and Jackson were in possession of military technology that still worked. That quieted any side conversations.

"I'm going to be completely honest with you. We don't know the status of the U.S. military. There are indications that some commanders, some units, have gone rogue. This technology can be traced back to the users. The last thing we want is to have renegade units of the U.S. military here."

It was Edna, the police receptionist, who answered that. "If they're coming, they would eventually be here anyway. At least this way, we'd know to be on the lookout, to be ready to defend ourselves."

"True, and we have taken precautions. Liam and Jackson won't use the devices until they are well into the desert."

Harper understood that what Tanda was describing was a stall tactic at best. Although the Chihuahuan desert was vast, there weren't very many towns. She remembered lying in the back seat of the jeep, Cade hovering at her side, and the desert scene flying by outside the window—miles and miles of nothing but scrub brush.

"You must have a plan, Tanda." Quinton Cooper, who Harper had met while walking home one afternoon, stood so he could be better heard. "Tell us what you need us to do, because we're not going to sit idly by while the Watchmen or anyone else takes what few supplies we have."

Tanda looked to Jackson, who stepped forward and explained a plan that had obviously been hammered out among the council. The citizens of Alpine that were assembled that October afternoon didn't merely hear the words.

They offered suggestions, amendments, words of caution.

It wasn't a confrontational discussion like those Harper had seen a hundred times before on national news between elected officials and their constituents. Instead, what she was watching was the give and take between those who were leading and those who had agreed to be led.

The group was like-minded. Any dissenting voices had either died, left, or chose to remain silent. Looking around, Harper saw in the faces of those around her a steely resolve and unanimous agreement.

And so it was decided. They would take the battle to the Watchmen two evenings hence, when the moon was new and the sky as dark as they were likely to get.

Thirty armed men and women would ride in vehicles. They would cram into panel vans and pickups beds and even a small school bus. They'd walk the final few miles. Tanda, Keme, Gonzo, Dixie, and Liam would each lead a group. Miles, Logan and Cade would prepare the triage center for injuries. One of them would accompany the groups headed to Mount Livermore. Harper glanced at Cade, but he simply shrugged. It hadn't been decided yet.

The rest of the council would oversee a reinforced perimeter barrier, just in case any of the Watchmen slipped through. In case something went wrong. For all they knew the Watchmen could be working with another group. Tanda reiterated that they would not leave the town, or those families staying behind, unguarded.

The meeting ended with a closing prayer by a man in a clergy collar. He was a large man, clean-shaven but with a tan that indicated he did more than sit in a church's office and prepare sermons.

Peggy once again leaned close to Harper and whispered, "That would be Pastor Tobias. Once worked for the Episcopal Church, but we've since become a very ecumenical community."

His voice, when he spoke was deep, rich, resonating. "I have no better words than that of our Irish brethren."

The crowd again quieted as Pastor Tobias raised a hand. "May the road rise up to meet you. May the wind be always at your back."

Harper was aware that all had stood. Jack backed up until he was standing in between Cade and Harper. Cade reached for the boy's hand, who nodded once and reached for Harper's hand. And Harper found that Olivia had squeezed between her and Peggy. Harper reached for Olivia's hand. The young girl smiled, then reached for Peggy's hand.

"May the sun shine warm upon your face; the rains fall soft upon your fields..."

Harper's mind thought of the family she'd acquired, of all they'd been through together, all they'd survived. Perhaps that explained their need to be pressed together, their absolute need for the physical contact and comfort of one another. Then she looked left, looked right, and realized the entire town of Alpine, those remaining after nearly five months in a world that they could not have imagined, were standing, holding hands, both drawing and supplying solace from and to one another.

"And until we meet again, may God hold you in the palm of His hand."

When they were back home, Harper helped put the children to bed, kissed Cade, and told him she needed a few minutes. She set the solar lantern to low and pulled out the spiral notebook, whose paper was more precious than all she had owned before. She closed her eyes and allowed her mind to comb back over the evening, Tanda's plan, the crowd's reaction, the pastor's blessing.

She had felt something in that moment that rose above the fear and exhaustion.

She'd felt hope.

And though she knew it might be transient, though she understood that there would be dark and seemingly hopeless nights ahead, she wanted to hold on to that moment a little longer. At least long enough to commit it to paper.

She began with the words Emily Dickinson had so aptly penned over one hundred fifty years earlier.

Hope is the thing with feathers,
That perches in the soul
And sings the tune without the words
And never stops at all.

Chapter 29

THINGS WENT BADLY FROM the beginning.

Cade opted to go with the advance team. Miles and Logan were more familiar with the trauma center, the interns, the process that now supplied emergency medicine to Alpine. Plus, Cade felt that he owed this community something.

Alpine was providing a haven for his family.

The least he could do was join in protecting it.

His decision to volunteer certainly wasn't from a sense of heroism or a need to do something historic. He simply felt he should, and he was learning that when he had a strong inclination toward or away from a thing he did well to listen—something he hadn't been good at before June 6th. But he could learn. He would learn.

The first problem was when the jeep broke down. Since there were only six people crammed into it, they were able to shuffle closer and fit them into the remaining vehicles.

The second problem was parking the vehicles and walking the final miles. Parking wasn't a problem. No one was on the roads. Gas had become increasingly scarce and people were, by and large, hunkered down at this point in their new existence. The problem was that a three-mile hike across a desert in the dark of a moonless night was much more difficult than a three-mile jog through the streets of Alpine. They lost a man to a turned ankle and a woman to a pulled Achilles tendon. Not wanting to slow everyone else down, they hobbled back toward the vehicles together.

Cade was with the advance team, which included Tanda, Jackson, and three others. Keme's team accompanied them. They stopped one mile out and deployed the spybot. Huddled together over the monitor, Cade was astounded at the clarity of the picture.

He'd forgotten the miracle that was technology.

The monitor only gave them a view of the area around the small clump of buildings. It couldn't see through walls although a jumble of heat signatures indicated that people were asleep in the buildings. It seemed that two men had pulled night duty.

Half a dozen horses were inside a corral positioned between the buildings and the rising, rocky slope that was Mt. Livermore. In fact, the fencing of the corral only covered three sides—the mountain's slope was steep enough and rocky enough to do the rest. No horse would willingly head up that rock face.

"Okay. Jackson, Cade, and Ron, I want you with me. We'll circle around the back where the horses are. Quinton, be ready with your men to walk the horses out. We don't want anyone escaping that way."

"And the cars?" Keme asked.

"I only see two. Give us time to move into position, then I want your group to disable those vehicles."

"How would you like me to do that, sister?"

"I'll leave that to you, brother."

The bantering helped to relieve the tension a little, but only a little.

Tanda pulled the radio from her pack and explained their plan to Liam, who was bringing up the second line of advance. "Give us two minutes to get into place, then I want half your people to empty out those three buildings. Drive them toward the west, where we'll be waiting. Stop anyone who tries to escape by whatever means necessary. Put the other half of your people spaced out around the perimeter to the north, west, and south."

"Ten-four."

They went in quietly, but that silence was shattered almost immediately.

Cade and Ron held back and released the horses while Tanda and Jackson moved to intercept the night guard. They'd managed to release half of the horses to Quinton's group when the relative quiet of the night was shattered by a rifle shot. Cade had reached for the halter of a gelding and the horse reared suddenly at the sound of the rifle. Three pops of a handgun quickly followed.

"I've got these," Ron growled. "Go!"

Cade didn't have to be told twice.

He was wearing a backpack filled with medical supplies, but he doubted that would be any use to someone suffering from multiple gunshot wounds. As he ran around the corner where he'd seen Tanda and Jackson disappear, he could hear shouting from behind them, followed by another gunshot.

If there was one thing he did know how to do, it was to ignore everything except for the patient in front of him. That had been drilled into him over many Saturday nights in the hospital's emergency room. He skidded around the corner. Tanda stood in an isosceles shooting stance. Her revolver was steady as was her voice as she said, "Jackson was hit."

Cade dropped beside Jackson, assessing the bullet wound in his chest, the amount of blood he'd lost, and the man's weak and thready pulse. Jackson gripped his hand, whispered, "Take care of her," and then he was gone.

Life—interrupted.

Completely.

Irrevocably.

Tanda flipped on her flashlight, shone it on Cade and Jackson. He shook his head, released Jackson's hand and stood. Tanda was holding the flashlight in her left hand and her service revolver in her right. She pointed the light at a dark shape on the ground. "I'm pretty sure he's gone too, but you better check."

Cade confirmed the night guard was dead.

He couldn't have said how many minutes had passed since they'd rounded the corner of the small compound—not many. Tanda's radio crackled with teams checking in.

"Horses are released."

"Cars are disabled."

A few minutes after that, as they cleared the barn and the area around the corral, Keme's voice came over Tanda's radio. "Everyone's assembled in the courtyard. We're doing a final sweep to pick up any stragglers."

"You're with me, Cade."

They walked around the corner of the building. There must have been a generator, because Keme had found mounted outdoor spotlights and turned them on. Their glare on the group assembled was relentless and unnatural.

Cade didn't know what he'd expected to see.

He had a fairly good idea of what he didn't expect to see, though.

Three boys, somewhere between ten and fifteen years of age, stood off to the side. Two of the men front and center had to be in their eighties, and there were at least three women nearly that old. One of the men was holding his right arm, which must have been grazed by a bullet. That explained the other gunshot he'd heard. The man was bleeding, but not profusely.

The majority of those assembled, and there were maybe two dozen, were what he had expected to see—middle-aged men, dirty, insolent, and unphased by this unexpected turn of events.

Tanda's voice was steady and authoritative.

Looking at her standing there in a renegade group's compound, in the dead of night, under the harsh spotlights, Cade would never have guessed that she was a small-town chief of police. Or that she'd just witnessed the death of a friend. Or that she'd moments before killed in self-defense.

What was obvious to everyone there was that she was deadly serious.

"If anyone here has been held against their wishes, if anyone would like to switch their allegiance, you have one chance to do that, and that chance is now."

At first no one moved, then the three boys stepped forward. It was the oldest boy who spoke. "They...they killed our parents, forced us to stay here and work for them."

Tanda nodded, then without turning around said, "Akule."

Her niece stepped forward, spoke to the boys in a low voice, and then ushered them away from the group.

Which left the bulk of the Watchmen standing there, defiant to the end, unimpressed by how quickly they'd been surrounded and disarmed.

"I know you." A middle-aged man with a tobacco-stained beard spit, barely managing to clear his boots. He must have been the other guard, as he was fully dressed. "You're that gal from Alpine. Whatcha going to do? Arrest us?" This produced some uneasy laughter from the group of reprobates.

"No. I don't have the officers needed to watch you or the supplies to feed you."

"Just going to kill us then...in cold blood? Always knew the law couldn't be trusted."

Cade thought that Tanda had complete control of her emotions, but something in her snapped. She stepped forward, grabbed the man by the front of his shirt, got right up into his face. "You killed those people in Van Horn, and how many others?"

"We only did what we had to in order to survive."

"And for that I would gladly put a bullet in your brain. It's called capital punishment, and I would be fully within the parameters of the law in times of civil unrest to do so since you just openly confessed to murder in front of a group of witnesses."

The man paled.

"You're not worth the bullet." She pushed him away and walked back to stand between Cade and Keme. "Instead, you're about to receive a lesson in another way to survive. Or not. That's totally up to you."

She explained their only option, and they listened—though Cade thought they looked unable or unwilling to believe what she was saying.

Then Tanda got on the radio and told the Alpine people who had stayed with the vehicles to drive them in. They reclaimed what the Watchmen had stolen, piled the goods in the back of the truck and the floor of the school bus. For the Watchmen, they left the barest of necessities. Keme confirmed the horses had been rounded up. He and half a dozen others would lead the pack back to Alpine.

"See you in a couple days, Sis." And then he was gone, vanishing into the night.

Ron confirmed that all of the vehicles had been permanently disabled. "We found a bit of fuel in canisters."

"Load that up too. The Watchmen won't be needing it."

"You can't do this." This from an older, frail-looking man.

He wasn't frail, though.

He was selfish, had committed unconscionable acts, and had chosen the wrong side.

"We'll die out here if you just leave us."

"It's only October. You have time to plant, and I suggest you start collecting water now. The dry spells can make things difficult."

"You're not leaving us a way to..." He licked his lips. "You're not leaving us a way out."

"Correct. I'm not." Her voice didn't soften exactly, but some of the harshness went out of her. She would explain to Cade later that there was no way to know who had been in charge and who had allowed themselves to be led down the wrong path. Was one as guilty as the other? She didn't know, and Cade didn't either.

"This isn't the world that was. You can't just take what belongs to others. You can't hope for a light sentence."

The sun hadn't risen but some of the darkness was fading from the sky.

"This land is harsh, but it will provide what you need to survive. The question is whether you have what it takes to make it. The question is whether you'll even try."

And then she walked away.

Jackson's body had been wrapped in a tarp and loaded into the back of one of the pick-ups. As they drove down the caliche road, the sun broke across the horizon. As they drove toward Alpine, Cade realized that this group and these people were both his present and his future.

Should he perish defending Alpine, as Jackson had, he would at least know that his and Harper's child, that Jack and Olivia and yes, even Harper, would be in a community that offered the best possible hope for years to come.

They wouldn't be easy years.

They might even be worse than this night had been. But at least no one in Alpine would face those challenges alone.

They had each other, and one way or another, that would be enough.

The End

from Veil of Destruction
   A Kessler Effect Novel, Book Three

A north wind tore across the Chihuahuan desert.

The snow that covered the surrounding mesas continued to fall, though more lightly, more softly than the day before. Most of the citizens of Alpine—what was left of them—remained burrowed in their beds. At least they had beds.

It was early, too early, to be out. But what Akule had to do was best done before the sun came up. Also, she didn't care to spend another sleepless night second-guessing her decision.

Akule had no doubt that her Aunt Tanda would be in her office. Tanda was the one person whose opinion she trusted. She trudged down the street, pushed open the door to the police station, and gave a small wave to Conor, who always seemed to be on the night shift.

"She back there?"

"Sure is."

"I'll just—" Akule waved toward the back, toward the office with *Police Chief* stenciled on the door. Conor nodded and went back to transcribing the previous day's call-outs in the journal Tanda insisted they keep. Of course, they weren't actual call-outs since no one's phone worked. A neighbor or family member would rush in asking for help and the officer on duty would respond. Everything went into the journal.

The world might have changed.

The apocalypse might have come.

But Tanda Lopez was determined to be the defender of law and order.

Akule tapped lightly on the door, then turned the knob.

Tanda's expression broke into a smile at the sight of her niece. "Wow. You're up early."

"So are you."

Tanda shrugged that away and rose to pull her into a hug.

Akule took the chair across from her. Now that she was here, she didn't know how to begin. Perhaps she should have simply left in the middle of the night. It would have been easier. Though she loved her aunt, and had no doubt that her aunt loved her, Tanda's piercing gaze caused her to squirm. Akule often wondered if Tanda had received their *abuela*'s second sight. She certainly seemed to know what a person was thinking before they spoke.

As if to prove that very point, Tanda sat back in her chair and cradled her mug of coffee. Her first words were a statement, not a question. "You're leaving."

"I have to go look for him."

Tanda continued to study her, as if assessing whether she was up to this task, then she nodded toward the window. "You could wait for the weather to clear."

"With no weather forecast, we have no idea when that will be."

"Why now?"

"Why not?"

"Where will you go?"

"I'll start in Cedar Hill. That's where he was living."

Tanda finally shifted her gaze, searched the opposite wall as if she could find the answer there. "I feel like I should go with you."

"You can't. We both know that. This town, what's left of it, depends on you."

"Paco is family. Family comes first." And then she surprised Akule with the confession, "We should have gone already. But it's been, you know…one hit after another."

First the battle with Marfa, then the battle with the Watchmen, then the winter and the flu season and even tighter rations.

"Dad won't want me to go. That's why I'm telling you."

"We'll tell him together."

"Do we have to?"

"Yeah. We do. He's on patrol at seven." Tanda glanced at the wall clock. Only five-thirty. "We can still catch him before his shift. Let's go."

They walked to the apartment that Keme had taken in Tanda's apartment building. He hadn't wanted to. He'd wanted to stay in the trailer that Akule and Paco had been raised in, the trailer where the memories of her mother still saturated every corner of every room. In the end, he'd seen the practicality of moving into town. That and the fact that a crazed and armed drifter had tried to break into Tanda's apartment. Tanda was fully capable of taking care of herself, but there'd been no stopping Keme then. He'd taken the apartment two doors down. He'd wanted Akule to move in with him, but she'd assured him she was fine with her roommates.

She was fine with her roommates.

But she needed to find her brother.

She hoped her father would understand that, but whether he did or not she was going.

Keme answered seconds after their knock, almost as if he'd been waiting for them. There had always been a strange kind of ESP between her dad and her aunt. She saw it now in the knowing glances they exchanged. She felt it in his sigh and Tanda's small shrug of her shoulders.

"Better come in."

They kept their coats on. The room was cold. Whoever had designed the building hadn't envisioned a time when there would be no heat or A/C. Open windows provided some relief in the summer, but during the winter...

Winter was simply a trial on one's spirit.

They sat around the dining room table. The occupants of the apartment had been caught out of town on June 6th.

The day the satellites stopped working.

The day their entire world changed.

It wasn't only a matter of cell phones not working. Nearly every aspect of their daily lives was dependent on 4G to one degree or another—shipping and receiving, manufacturing, GPS and signal lights, air traffic control towers, even train schedules. The train crash that had occurred that first day still lay across the tracks that wound through Alpine, a constant reminder to the day that everything changed.

"I'm going to find Paco."

"No, you're not."

"I am."

"We've talked about this. We agreed to wait until spring."

"I'm not waiting."

Akule's great-grandmother had been Kiowa. What percentage, Akule didn't know. Things like Ancestry.com no longer existed. Abuela had looked Indian. She had acted Indian. She had the stoicism of the Native Americans and the stubbornness of the Hispanic people. Abuela was old and diabetic and had been one of the first casualties.

But Akule saw her great-grandmother's traits in her father, and she felt those same traits in herself. They were like two trains colliding, neither willing or able to change course. She was reminded again of the freight train and the Amtrak train. One had sideswiped the other. Their timing had been off by only a few seconds. The resulting crash had killed eight and injured more.

Fortunately, Tanda weighed in. "I'm sure you two could do this all day, but I need to get back to work, Keme has patrol, and Akule...well, I'm not sure what you were supposed to do today."

"Helping Doc Cade, but I already told him I wouldn't be there."

"You told him you were leaving?" Keme sat back, raised and then lowered his hands as if to say *can you believe this girl*?

"I would like to side with you on this Keme." Tanda cupped her hands, breathed into them, then stuck them in the pockets of her coat. "I don't like the idea of her going—"

"She's not."

"Or of her going alone."

"Definitely not."

"But I feel it too." Tanda sat forward. For a moment she stared down at the table, as if she might find the answers there. She shook her head once, then glanced from Keme to Akule. "I feel it too. Someone needs to go, and I don't...I just don't see how I can."

"Why now? Why not wait until spring?"

Akule was ready with her list of reasons. "There will be more people on the roads in the spring. There will be more danger in the spring. You said yourself that the roads are basically empty right now. We haven't had a drifter in what...a month?"

"Doesn't mean they aren't out there."

"I can take care of myself, dad."

Keme exploded out of his chair, paced the short distance to the living area and back. "How would you even get there?"

"I'll take my mare."

"You'll need a pack animal too. You'll need grain for the mare and supplies for yourself." Tanda sat back, crossed her arms, stuck her hands under her armpits as if to warm them.

"It's a long trip, Akule. I know you're strong. You've matured a lot in the last six months, and if anyone can find Paco *and his family*..." She emphasized the last three words, as if Akule had forgotten about her two nephews and sister-in-law. "If anyone can find them, I believe you can. But travelling five hundred miles on horseback in the dead of winter won't be easy."

"I don't expect it to be."

"Say you can make thirty miles a day, that's a little more than two weeks there and two weeks back. Plus, you can't bring them back on your horse."

"And you're not even sure he'll be there." Keme sat again, concern and heartache coloring his expression.

Akule understood what that was about.

She understood that her father had lost his grandmother, his wife, and countless friends. Maybe he thought it was better to hold on to the one child he had with him rather than risk her being killed in the search for the rest of his family. He might have felt that way, but that wasn't what he said.

"You think I don't want to go? You think I wouldn't have left the day we understood nothing was going back to normal? Or the day your mother died?" He dropped his head, and that sign of resignation tore at Akule's heart more than his words. Finally he raised his gaze to hers. "The safest thing, the smartest thing is to wait here. Paco knows where we are. He'll get here when he can."

"I can't wait for that, dad. I can't do the safe thing. What's the point in trying so hard to stay alive if we're not going to at least attempt to save the people we love?"

Keme didn't have an answer to that.

Tanda rubbed her temples with her fingertips.

"Headache?" Akule asked.

Tanda waved away the question and addressed her next comment to Keme. "We can't stop her. She'll go with or without your permission. She's only telling us because she respects you."

Akule didn't like being talked about as if she wasn't there, but she also appreciated Tanda stating the obvious. She would go—with or without her father's permission.

Then Tanda played the card that hit home. "Lucy would agree with her. In fact, she would have insisted that you go months ago. I know it, and you know it."

All of the argument went out of her dad at the mention of her mother's name. "Fine."

Akule breathed out a sigh of relief.

"But I'm going with you."

"Dad, I don't need you with me. I don't want you with me."

"It doesn't matter what you want, Akule. I'm going."

Tanda nodded as if she'd expected as much. Why hadn't Akule seen this coming? She should have simply left town. She could be five miles north by now. Five miles closer to her brother.

But another voice, a smaller voice pushed to the front of her thoughts. It said, *why not go with your dad? Why do you feel a need to do this alone?* She didn't have an answer for that voice.

"Forty-eight hours," Tanda said. "Let me see what supplies I can get from Stan, and what kind of pack animal. You can both ride your mares. Take something to trade for two more horses once you get there. That should be enough. The kids are still small enough that they can ride with Paco and Claire."

Tanda stood, as if it was settled.

They all stood.

It was settled. She'd leave in forty-eight hours, and she wouldn't be going alone.

Akule's father surprised her then. He pulled her into his arms, then reached out and pulled Tanda into the circle. They stood there, the three of them, and Akule understood that she would hold onto this image until she was back in Alpine again. And she was coming back. But she'd come back with her brother, his wife, and both their children. She wasn't going to settle for anything less.

Veil of Destruction, available on Amazon.

A UTHOR'S NOTE

This book is dedicated to my 10th grade English teacher, Peggy Looper. She had a passion for words, for stories, and for understanding how they reflect and shape our world.

I visited and thoroughly researched Alpine, Texas and the surrounding locations mentioned in this book. Any changes made within the pages of this book were done so in order to expedite the plot of the book. In 1978, NASA scientist Donald J. Kessler published a paper titled, "Collision Frequency of Artificial Satellites: The Creation of a Debris Belt." This paper described a cascading collision of lower orbital satellites, something that has since been termed the Kessler Effect or the Kessler Syndrome. I have done my best to adequately present his theories within the text of this story. Any errors made in that representation are my own.

Many people were helpful in the writing of this book, including Kristy Kreymer, Tracy Luscombe, Judith Ann Oliver McGhee, and Matt Walter.

Teresa Lynn, thank you for making every book better.

Joyce and Bruce, you are always an inspiration.

Donna and Dorsey, thank you for hiking Guadalupe Peak with me. I'll never forget how we saved one another on the hike down.

And, of course, Bob—I love you, babe.

Vannetta Chapman is the USA To-
day and Publishers Weekly best-
selling author of over 40 books
in a variety of genres that include
dystopian, suspense, romantic sus-
pense, romance, and cozy mystery. She was an English teacher
at the high school and collegiate level for fifteen years. She currently resides in the Texas Hill Country where she writes full
times. For more information, visit her at her website.

Share your thoughts with Vannetta via the contact button on
her webpage.

For information about book sales and future releases here, sign
up for her newsletter here.

amazon.com/Vannetta-Chapman/e/B003TCO9N0/ref=dp_byline_cont_pop_ebooks_1

bookbub.com/profile/vannetta-chapman

facebook.com/VannettaChapmanBooks

goodreads.com/vannettachapman

instagram.com/vannettachapman/

pinterest.com/vannettachapman/

https://twitter.com/VannettaChapman

A LSO BY VANNETTA CHAPMAN

Kessler Effect Series
Veil of Mystery, Prequel
Veil of Anarchy, Book 1
Veil of Confusion, Book 2
Veil of Destruction, Book 3

Defending America Series
Coyote's Revenge
Roswell's Secret

Standalone Novel
Security Breach

See a complete booklist at
https://vannettachapman.com/book-list/